THE PRIMROSE

It seemed so innocent when the Earl of Warrington invited Arabella to go for an early morning horseback ride. Then, far from the manor, Miles asked if she would like to dismount for a stroll through a pretty wooded area.

She could not resist this charming idea. Taking her hand in his, Miles led her along a narrow path with primrose on either side. Then, when they were out of sight of any prying eyes, he placed a hand on each of her shoulders and drew her close.

Arabella could feel his breath as it mingled with hers in the cool morning air.

"I've waited a long time to do this, my dear," he said softly, just before his lips came down on hers. . . .

IRENE SAUNDERS, a native of Yorkshire, England, spent a number of years exploring London while working for the U.S. Air Force there. A love of travel brought her to New York City, where she met her husband, Ray, then settled in Miami, Florida. She now lives in Port St. Lucie, Florida, dividing her time between writing, bookkeeping, gardening, needlepoint, and travel.

The Colonel's Campaign

Irene Saunders

A SIGNET BOOK

SIGNET
Published by the Penguin Group
Penguin Books USA Inc., 375 Hudson Street,
New York, New York, 10014 U.S.A.
Penguin Books Ltd, 27 Wrights Lane, London W8 5TZ, England
Penguin Books Australia Ltd, Ringwood, Victoria, Australia
Penguin Books Canada Ltd, 2801 John Street, Markham, Ontario,
Canada L3R 1B4
Penguin Books (N.Z.) Ltd, 182-190 Wairau Road,
Auckland 10, New Zealand

Penguin Books Ltd, Registered Offices:
Harmondsworth, Middlesex, England

First published by Signet, an imprint of Penguin Books USA Inc.

First Printing, June, 1990

10 9 8 7 6 5 4 3 2 1

 REGISTERED TRADEMARK—MARCA REGISTRADA

BOOKS ARE AVAILABLE AT QUANTITY DISCOUNTS WHEN USED TO PROMOTE
PRODUCTS OR SERVICES. FOR INFORMATION PLEASE WRITE TO PREMIUM
MARKETING DIVISION, PENGUIN BOOKS USA INC., 375 HUDSON STREET,
NEW YORK, NEW YORK 10014.

1

March, 1815

The front door of Warrington House slammed loudly, caught, no doubt, by a blustery north wind. Then came the sound of booted feet being stamped hard to rid them of much of their dirt before entering the rather shabby-looking breakfast room.

Sir George Wetherby's kindly face lit with genuine pleasure as his nephew appeared in the doorway. "Ah, there you are at last, my boy. You must have been up and out early this morning, for I'd swear it was not yet light when I heard the front door close behind you."

He reached for the coffeepot, refilled his own cup, and poured another for Miles as the younger man limped across the room and took his place at the head of the large mahogany table. Hooking his cane over the back of the chair to his left, Miles ran his fingers through his black hair to repair the damage the wind had wrought.

"There's much to be done at this time of year, George, as you well know, and the days are not yet long enough to complete it all," he said with a sigh, then he glanced up at the manservant who was hovering behind his chair. "I believe I've worked up quite an appetite, Thomas. You can get me a kipper to start with, I think, and then some of the ham, eggs, and a little kedgeree, if you please."

He helped himself to a slice of toast and was buttering it when his uncle cleared his throat loudly. It was a signal, he knew, that Sir George was about to say something but was waiting until the old butler had served him and left the room before beginning.

Thomas had been with Miles' family all of his life, and had now reached an age and position where he could take his time about his duties without incurring the slightest reproach. Only the best was good enough for his young master, and so he minutely inspected every piece of food before placing it upon the plate.

Miles looked across at his uncle with an understanding smile, sympathizing with the other man's impatience to impart some piece of local news.

When at last the food was arranged to Thomas' satisfaction and placed in front of the master, Miles grinned and gave his usual nod of approval. Only then did the old servant walk slowly from the room, closing the door firmly behind him.

Sir George leaned forward, unable to contain himself a moment longer. "Did you hear that there's to be a burial at the church this afternoon, Miles? Never met the fellow myself, and never wanted to, but I understand he was once a friend of yours."

Miles Cavendish, Earl of Warrington, gave him a quizzical look and waited. He was fond of his Uncle George, and much aware of the pleasure the older man derived from recounting interesting local happenings. Some might have called it gossip, but they would have been unkind, for, having lived most of his life in the city, Sir George was fascinated by what went on in and around the village, and he was the first to offer help when it was needed. The villagers were all fond of the tall, gray-haired gentleman who took such an interest in their well-being.

"Sir Richard Barton got himself killed in a duel, I understand," Sir George went on, watching his nephew's face as he spoke and noting the look of painful surprise that came into the silver-gray eyes. He shook his head sadly, for there was worse yet to come. "Word is that he was caught cheating at cards and challenged his accuser."

"Was it pistols?" Miles asked, laying down his fork. When his uncle nodded, he added, "He never was a good shot, but if he was the challenger, then his opponent had the choice. Rumor had it that he was making his living at card play, for his father had little to leave him except for the old house in which his sister, Clarice, now resides."

He looked with distaste at the food on his plate and wondered vaguely why Thomas had brought him so much. He had no appetite these days, not the way he had some seven or more years ago when he and Richard frequently went off fishing or hunting together. They would return to a nearby inn for a hearty supper, washed down with the best wine in the cellar; then, with a bottle of brandy on the table between them, they would place bets on which of them would get the prettiest one of the barmaids.

It had been just a game to Miles, for there was usually little to choose between the girls, but Richard had always been a sore loser. They had agreed at the outset that money must not be used as an enticement, but despite this, Richard would frequently get the prettier one alone where he thought he was unobserved, and offer her coins to favor him the most.

"And did he cheat at cards?" Sir George asked curiously.

The sound of his uncle's voice brought Miles back to the present. "I'm sorry, George, I was far away," he said, smiling apologetically.

"I asked you if he did cheat at cards," his uncle repeated, "for it's a wonder he lasted so long if it was his habit."

"He cheated when we were youngsters and got a sound thrashing for it once, as I recall," Miles told him, remembering the occasion quite clearly, "but I should think he either stopped or else became more skillful at it." He pushed the plate of food away from him. "I'm afraid I'm not as hungry as I thought," he murmured. "Would you mind passing me the coffeepot, George?"

They sat in silence for a while, the older man not wishing

to disturb his nephew, who was quite obviously deep in thought.

Finally, Sir George took a last sip from his cup, dabbed at his mouth with his napkin, and cleared his throat. "I'm going into Worksop this afternoon, Miles. Is there anything I can get for you while I'm there?"

Miles looked up blankly, then shook his head as if to disperse his thoughts. "I'm sorry," he said, "I must have been dreaming again. There are a few things I need from town if it's no bother. I'll make a list before I go out." With an almost automatic gesture he massaged the thigh of his bad leg as though to ease the tense muscles, then he rose and reached for his cane, standing for a moment and looking across at his uncle. "It's a good thing his father is already gone, or it would have broken the old man's heart," he said with a sad shake of his head, then made his way slowly out of the room.

As Miles had told his uncle, there was much work to be done, for it was March already, and though it was still quite cold, the ground had begun to soften slightly after the harsh winter. He spent an hour or so with his bailiff, going over a list of repairs that were needed on the outbuildings and some of the farm workers' cottages, then he called for his horse and rode out to assess the damages for himself.

By early afternoon he found himself in the vicinity of the church. He rode around to the back, tied his horse to a tree, then climbed over the stile into the graveyard. He made his way carefully over the uneven ground between the graves until he reached the newly dug hole in the section where the Bartons were buried. He looked up as he heard voices and saw two workmen waiting near the church wall, their shovels dropped carelessly on the ground, rubbing their red hands together and stamping their feet to keep out the cold as they waited to complete their task.

A chill wind whistled past the tall elms that stood like sentinels guarding the old stone slabs, and Miles turned up the collar of his heavy coat. Then he stepped over to a cluster of trees just far enough away for him to see the mourners when they came out of the church without intruding his presence upon them. He hooked his cane on a branch behind him, leaned against a solid tree trunk, and waited.

He was just paying his respects to a man he had once known, he told himself. A man with whom he had played as a boy and later had gone fishing and shooting with and to local balls and parties, but who had disgraced himself by running off, just five years ago, with Lady Arabella, the only child of Lord Darnley.

She's a widow now, a voice inside him said. What is she like? Has she changed much from the eighteen-year-old you thought you knew so well? Is she still as beautiful as she was when she jilted you to elope with Richard?

There were sounds from the direction of the church, and Miles looked up to see a small procession coming out: first the pallbearers carrying the coffin, then the vicar, and after him, the mourners followed slowly behind.

He easily recognized Arabella despite the heavy veil that completely covered her chestnut curls, for there was something about the way she walked, held her head perhaps, that was painfully familiar. Then, just as he thought he would not get a chance to see her face, she left the footpath and started to walk between the graves, throwing back her veil to better see where she trod.

He almost gasped, for though the years had dealt harshly with him, they had treated her more kindly. There was not the least doubt of it. She was every bit as lovely as she had been before, but in a different way. The eager, happy girl had gone, and in her place was a very beautiful woman with large, sad blue eyes that shed not a single tear as she stood by the graveside in her garb of somber black.

The coffin was lowered into the ground and the vicar's voice droned on, repeating the words of the all-too-familiar service. Miles watched as Arabella stooped to pick up some earth and drop it down upon the coffin. She turned away as the other two mourners took her place, and then she glanced up, looking directly at Miles as he stood, hat in hand, still leaning slightly against the tree.

He saw a glimmer of recognition in those lovely eyes, and something else that he could not put a name to, then she looked down and dropped her veil as she turned to where Richard's sister, Clarice, and her husband, Sir Brian Summerson, the only other mourners, waited. It had turned into a bitterly cold day, for the sun had made but a fleeting appearance and the strong wind was still blowing from the north. Sir Brian put his hat back upon his head, stamped his feet, rubbed his hands together, and then hurried the ladies to the waiting coach.

Not until they were out of sight did Miles replace his hat, collect his cane, and walk slowly over to the grave, looking down into it for a moment before reaching for a handful of earth and throwing it in. Then he turned, nodding to the gravediggers as they hurried to finish their work.

He retrieved his horse and rode off, and it was fortunate that the gelding knew its way home, for its master was in too deep thought to notice where he went.

2

March, 1816

"You want to leave here and go up to London? Why on earth would you want to do that?" Lady Clarice Summerson asked, her voice squeaking loudly at the very idea. "We may not have looked after you the way your papa could—if he'd wanted to have aught to do with you, that is—but you've not lacked for anything despite the fact that you came to us completely without funds. From the look of those fancy gowns you were so anxious to throw away, my poor brother must have spent every penny he had on you."

Arabella glanced at her sister-in-law, who was only ten years older than her own twenty-four years, but could have easily been taken for a fifty-year-old. Clarice had never endeavored to make the best of herself; she could conceivably have once been quite attractive if she had, for she possessed the same pale-blue eyes and light blond hair as her brother, Richard, but there the resemblance ended, for Clarice's lips were constantly set in a thin line of discontent. Perhaps to compensate, she ate greedily, and this showed in her considerable girth, for though she was small in stature she must have weighed in the region of thirteen stones.

In the year Arabella had lived here, she had never quarreled with the only close family Richard had, and she refused to do so now. There was no doubt about it: she had been completely without funds after paying for Richard's funeral. Two days ago she had been forced to sell the few small pieces of jewelry she owned in order to buy her ticket to London on the stagecoach.

It had at first been quite a surprise to Arabella when Richard's sister and her husband had been most insistent that she stay with them after Richard's death. It was not until later that she found out the reason why. Richard's heir, a quite distant cousin, had apparently written to her saying she might stay in the house undisturbed as long as she wished. But the letter had not reached her, for Sir Brian had seen it first and replied on her behalf.

The property, consisting of little more than the house and grounds, was entailed. Sir Brian knew this, but he had eagerly "bought" it from Richard some years before for a large sum of money and an agreement that he and Clarice could live there for the rest of their lives, or until Richard's death. Richard had no desire to put down roots, but enjoyed the freedom of going wherever an opportunity to gamble might take him and his less enthusiastic bride.

The money had not lasted long, of course, but had gone the way of all Richard's money: to pay gambling debts or to stake him in the next game.

"If your father has not forgiven you in all these years, it's not likely he'll take you back now, you know," Clarice continued, with a sniff. "Though what's to forgive about marrying a fine young man like my brother, I'll never know. Richard once told me you had a rare temper when you got started. That Lord Cavendish you were betrothed to would never have stood for it, you know."

"I'm going to London to visit my aunt," Arabella said patiently, for what must have been the tenth time in two days. "It is mere coincidence that my father just happens to be staying with her at the moment."

As she spoke she glanced around the slightly shabby drawing room, which had not been refurbished since

Richard's mother had come here as a bride. For the last year it had been made to seem even more drab by the wide black ribbons that Clarice had insisted on draping around all the paintings and windows both here and in the dining room as symbols of mourning for her dead brother. The furniture was good, however, and if the new owner had it re-covered, it could conceivably look elegant once more.

Arabella had known the house for years, but only from the outside. When she first saw the interior a year ago, she had been glad that Richard had not desired to live here, for he would never have hung on to enough of his winnings to turn it into a bright, cheerful home. But it had been somewhere to stay during the twelve months of mourning, and now her only wish was that, once she boarded the stage for London, she might never see the inside of the house again.

Sir Brian came into the room, helped himself to a cup of cold tea and a scone, and settled back in one of the armchairs.

"Is she staying, then?" he asked his wife, nodding in Arabella's direction.

Clarice sighed heavily. "She thinks of only herself, my dear, and does not care anything about us. I just don't know what Richard was thinking of when he married her."

"Has that fellow been around again looking for her?"

Arabella had been about to excuse herself and go upstairs, as she usually did when Clarice and her husband started their distasteful habit of discussing her as though she were not in the room. Now, however, she leaned back in her chair, curious to hear what fellow Sir Brian was speaking of.

"I don't know who you mean," Clarice said repressively, trying to catch his eye and stop him saying more, but her husband was busily buttering the scone and did not look up.

"The one she was betrothed to, of course," he mumbled, frowning and brushing at his knees as some crumbs dropped onto his breeches. "You told me he was here the other day, and has been here two or three times before."

"I don't know what you're talking about," Clarice responded a little shrilly, "and I just remembered I have something I must do upstairs at once."

She got up to leave, but Arabella was quicker. She was

at the door before her sister-in-law, slipping a hand through her arm and saying a little too sweetly, "I think I'll come with you, Clarice, for I find myself intrigued to learn that someone has been inquiring about me and I have not been informed."

Clarice swung around. "Now see what you've done, Brian," she said angrily. "It was bad enough him being there at the funeral, but he should have known better than to come calling on a widow in mourning."

Arabella had schooled herself to keep her temper under control for a whole year, but now she could do so no longer. "Are you saying that Miles Cavendish has called here several times to convey his condolences to me, and you have kept me uninformed of this?" she asked in a voice that was dangerously quiet.

"It wasn't right for him to come alone like that, asking to see you," Clarice said huffily. "I saw him myself and told him that you were devastated at your loss and unable to see anyone, which is what you would have been if you'd felt about Richard the way you should."

"How many times has he called, and when?" Arabella asked sharply.

"Three, maybe four," her sister-in-law said grudgingly. "He came about a month after the funeral, and a couple of times after that. Then he called a week ago."

As Arabella let go of her arm, Clarice started to rub it, then asked peevishly, "What do you want with a cripple, anyway?"

"A cripple? What do you mean? Has he been injured recently?"

Clarice smiled with glee as she saw the concern in Arabella's eyes. "Why are you so worried? You didn't want him when he was whole, never mind now," she taunted.

Sir Brian, becoming a little exasperated, spoke up. "He went to fight with Wellington just after you and Richard were wed, and he returned about six months before Richard died. He received the leg wound, so they say, just about when the war ended the first time, and he had been in hospital for months before he came back here."

Arabella looked slowly from one to the other of them. There was nothing to be gained by recriminations, for they couldn't help what they were, but she wished now that she had not listened to them but gone to London a year ago, right after the funeral. She turned on her heel and went upstairs to the bedchamber she had been using for the last twelve months, closing the door and locking it behind her.

Crossing the room, she sank wearily into the chair in front of the dressing table, grateful for the privacy the room afforded. Out of the corner of her eye she saw a movement, then felt a soft paw tap lightly against her leg. Snowball, her three-year-old white Persian cat, was asking permission to jump onto her lap. Once he was settled and purring happily, she allowed herself to think again, calmly this time, of Miles' several visits.

Would it have made any difference if she had been told he wished to see her? She would certainly not have turned him away, but it would have been an embarrassing meeting.

She had often thought of him standing there watching the burial, and she wondered what thoughts were passing through his mind. He had not looked annoyed, but she readily acknowledged that he had every right to be very angry with her indeed.

She had been not quite eighteen when she was promised to him by her father, and though no formal announcement had been made, the papers were signed and everything set for them to be married toward the end of the summer. She had raised no objections to marrying him, for she had none. In fact, she was happy about it, for she had known him for years, liked him as a friend, and had begun to feel a delightful warmth inside and a breathlessness when he looked at her in a certain way. Even now her heart fluttered at the memory of that look in his eyes.

If only he had touched her, taken her into his arms, and, perhaps, kissed her, she now knew that Richard would never have stood a chance. But Miles was too much of a gentleman for that. He had been waiting, she realized, until their betrothal was announced and his ring was upon her finger.

The late date had been picked because of her foolish

insistence that she must have her first Season in London before being tied down in marriage. What a little brat she must have been at eighteen!

Well, she didn't get her Season in London, after all, but she had no one to blame except herself—and Richard, of course.

Snowball's ears pricked up and he looked toward the door, then up at his mistress. Arabella could see the knob turning before a sharp rap sounded on the door itself and Clarice called loudly, ''Arabella, open this door at once. I wish to speak further with you.''

Arabella rose a little wearily and walked across the room to open the door, the cat still in her arms. ''What is it you want, Clarice? Surely everything of worth has already been said,'' she suggested hopefully while nevertheless moving aside to allow her sister-in-law to enter.

''You know I cannot tolerate cats,'' Clarice snapped pettishly. ''Lock him in the armoire at once, for if he leaps upon me, you know I'll have the vapors.''

Arabella shook her head firmly. ''You'll not have to worry about him for much longer, for he's coming with me to London, of course. Sit over there,'' she said, pointing to the only chair in the chamber, ''and I'll sit on the bed and keep a tight hold of him.''

With a loud sniff, Clarice sat down heavily, and the small chair made a slight creak as her weight descended upon it. She looked down at the legs as though expecting them to give way at any moment, then said accusingly, ''If you've broken any furniture, you owe it to us to have it repaired before you leave, for out of the goodness of our hearts, we've given you and that animal food and shelter for a whole year and asked for nothing in return.''

The phrase had been repeated too many times lately for Arabella to be anything else but amused. After all, it had been only at their insistence that she had stayed with them. ''That chair does not squeak when I sit on it,'' she said, trying to keep a straight face, but the twinkle in her eyes gave her away.

"I may be a little more rounded than I used to be," Clarice snapped, "but Sir Brian prefers a lady to be that way. If you're going to London to try to find yourself another husband, you'll not succeed unless you put some more flesh on your bones."

For a moment Arabella thought that her sister-in-law had finally accepted the fact that she really was leaving in the morning, but her hopes were quickly dashed.

"Sir Brian is going to write a letter to my cousin, Richard's heir, for your signature, telling him that you have no funds and nowhere to go, and asking if you might stay here for at least another year, or until you are able to make other arrangements. He doesn't need the house, so if Sir Brian words it the right way, he'll just have to agree," she declared firmly.

Arabella looked at her in amazement. "Clarice," she said slowly, knowing that Sir Brian was quite capable of appending her signature to the letter himself, "I've made it quite clear that I'm leaving in the morning for London."

"You don't care about anyone except yourself, do you?" Clarice snapped. "We paid Richard a generous sum of money to live here for the rest of our lives, and if it has all been spent, then as his wife it's just as much your fault as his. I know that he would have expected you to help us stay here. Once the letter is written and my cousin has agreed, you don't have to actually live with us if you don't want to. In fact, we'd much prefer to have the house to ourselves for a change."

"Would it not look rather strange if I should run into your cousin, Viscount Barton, at some social event?" Arabella asked a trifle sarcastically.

Clarice looked askance. "Surely you do not intend to go out socially just twelve months after my brother's death? We'll be in half-mourning for another year yet, and so should you. I've no doubt your aunt will set you straight, however, as you are quite obviously unaware of how to go along."

Arabella rose. "I've no doubt she will," she said dryly, "but whether I socialize or not, you may tell Sir Brian that

I have no intention of appending my signature to any letter he writes. And now I believe that Snowball has certain needs and I'll have to release him in a moment.''

Her sister-in-law rose abruptly. "Don't you dare put him down until I'm out of this room," she snapped as she hurried toward the door, "and I'll tell Sir Brian how uncooperative you are. I've no doubt he'll want to talk to you himself after dinner."

When the door closed behind Clarice, Arabella sighed with relief. Then she released the squirming cat, who went to sniff delicately all around the chair on which her sister-in-law had been sitting. They would both be happy when they were in Tom Benson's cart tomorrow morning and on their way to the stage, though she had no illusions as to the discomfort of the journey to London. She had been forced to use that means of travel to get here after Richard had died, and her stomach had not yet forgotten the odors emanating from the other passengers and the food they had brought along with them.

There was a knock on the door and one of the maids entered.

"The master must have missed this one when he picked up the post, miss," she said, "so I thought I'd bring it up and see if there's anything I can do for you. We'll all be sorry to see you go, and Cook said I was to tell you that she'll pack a little something for you to eat on the way."

"Thank you, Molly. I'll stop into the kitchen to say good-bye to everyone before I leave," Arabella said softly, reaching out a hand for the letter. "I'll miss them all, I know." Thanks were all she could offer for the many kindnesses she had received from them, but it would be enough, she knew.

As the maid closed the door, Arabella glanced down at the letter and gave a little gasp. It had not been franked, and was addressed to her in exactly the same way as the others she had received.

The first had come before Richard's body had scarce cooled, and was carefully printed and unsigned. The unknown writer expressed joy at her husband's death and told her she must now pay for his sins. Then a second one arrived a week after the burial. She found it on the hall table and it was longer than the first. It said that her enticements were as much to blame as her husband's cheating and that her time would come.

With trembling fingers she broke the seal and unfolded the sheet of paper. The words, in large block letters as before, seemed to jump off the sheet: "YOU CAN'T HIDE THERE FOREVER. YOU WILL BE FOUND NO MATTER WHERE YOU RUN."

With the note still clutched in her hand, she sat down on the bed and tried to stop shaking. Who could be doing this to her, and why? And how could they know that she was leaving?

After a while she got up and went over to the dressing table. Opening a drawer, she withdrew the writing case her father had given her on her sixteenth birthday. Carefully hidden at the back were the other letters she had received, and she took them out and compared them with this latest one. There was no doubt that it was the same hand, but none of them gave her an inkling as to who could have sent them.

Folding them carefully, she replaced them in the case but did not put it back into the drawer, for soon now she would be packing it into her portmanteau with her clothes and the rest of her meager possessions.

Suddenly, she felt the need to go outside. The room was stifling and she just had to get out, go for a walk and breathe some fresh air into her lungs. She was still wearing her outdoor shoes, so she hurriedly flung a cloak around her shoulders and left the room, making her way down the back stairs, for she did not want any more confrontations with her in-laws.

Taking long, easy strides, she walked down the lane leading to the village, then took the shortcut across some fields that would take her past Darnley Hall, her old home. She had no idea of stopping, though she knew there was no danger of coming across her father, for he was still in London. All she wanted to do was to take a last look at the old house before she left the neighborhood tomorrow.

She did not see the horse and rider until they were almost upon her, then she stepped quickly out of their way, but it was too late, for it was Miles Cavendish, and he had seen her.

"Good afternoon, Arabella," he said, turning back and doffing his hat to reveal the thick mass of unruly black hair she remembered so well. "How have you been? I called on several occasions, but Lady Summerson said you were unable to see anyone."

"I'm very well, thank you, Miles," she said softly, her cheeks turning to a deep crimson as she remembered the last time she had heard that deep, husky voice. It had been just before leaving for London so many years ago. "My sister-in-law did not realize, I'm afraid, that I would have been most pleased to see any of my old friends who stopped by."

His smile was warm and his gray eyes kindly as he looked down from his seat on the chestnut gelding.

"I just wanted to say how sorry I was about Richard, and to tell you also that if I can ever be of assistance, you need not fear to ask," he said gently.

"Thank you, Miles. I'll remember that." Her voice was so soft that it was almost a whisper. "It was good of you to come last year to the burial."

He thought she had never looked so lovely, the hood of the black cape framing her chestnut hair and delicate features. "I just happened to be near the churchyard at the time, so I thought I would at least pay my respects, but I did not want to disturb the family."

She smiled faintly. "I don't think they would have even noticed."

"Are you warm enough?" he asked. "I could take you up in front if you'd like to get back more quickly than walking."

She shook her head. "I came out for fresh air and exercise more than anything else. But it is kind of you to offer."

He nodded. "My pleasure," he said; then, as she seemed to have temporarily lost her tongue, he added, "I hope to see you again soon."

She did not reply, but just looked at him, almost wishing

he would scold her for what she had done, and get it over with.

Instead, he replaced his hat, then with a wave he turned and went off at a trot in the direction of his home.

Arabella shrugged slightly, then turned toward her old home. She'd skirt it and make her way back through the village.

It had been a shock to meet him suddenly like that, but at least he had gone out of his way to show her that he did not bear her any ill will for the dreadful thing she had done to him.

In a way she regretted now that she was leaving tomorrow, for she had missed the only chance she might ever have to tell him how sorry she was that she had treated him so badly. She had known long before she reached Gretna Green that she had made a dreadful mistake, that she felt nothing for Richard and was more than a little in love with Miles, but it had been too late then.

Miles had not gone far before he turned to look back. There was a serious expression on his face as he watched her stride off in the direction of Darnley Hall. She had always loved to walk the countryside, moving at a brisk pace, enjoying the feel of the wind and sun caressing her cheeks. He remembered how, when she was not yet eighteen, he and Richard seemed to frequently run into her when they were out riding, and they would, of course, stop for a word.

He had always offered to take her up then, and she usually refused, but in the dim recesses of his memory he was now hearing something else that he had long ago forgotten.

It was Richard's challenging voice, saying, "No, I'll take her up in front of me, Miles. Give a fellow a chance, can't you? You'll have her to yourself soon enough when you're married."

Then Arabella, tossing her head and starting to walk away, said, "I'll not ride back with either one of you. I came out for some fresh air and I'd sooner walk back."

Richard was swooping low now, trying to clasp her around the waist, and Arabella was neatly evading him and moving in among the bushes, determined to walk as she'd set out to do.

She had shown no sign whatever then of preferring Richard, and it had never occurred to Miles that his friend was jealous of him.

He turned the gelding in the direction of home once more and wondered, not for the first time, just what had really happened six years ago, after Arabella had left Darnley Hall and started out for London.

3

The drawing room at Warrington House had deteriorated deplorably from the elegant showplace it had been in the day when Miles' mother was alive and entertained the gentle folk of half the county. But she had been gone some fifteen years now, having neglected a putrid throat and succumbed to a disease of the lungs.

For the next three years, the earl and young Miles had been kept in hand somewhat by Jennifer, Miles' sister who was the older by two years, but once she married and settled in Northumberland, the entire house had been neglected. After all, what did two men care if the curtains were becoming faded and the upholstery worn? They simply made themselves comfortable by moving in some of the man-size leather chairs from the library. And when their two favorite retrievers, allowed indoors for the first time, swept some of the ornaments onto the floor and broke them, they told the housekeeper to put them all away, for who needed such fripperies all over the place?

It was not long before Miles was alone in the house, except for the dogs, for his father's favorite hunter balked at a jump one day, sending the earl over a hedge and breaking his neck. Concentrating on keeping up the estates and training a new bailiff, Miles had scarcely noticed when the old housekeeper retired and a new, less caring one took her place. If it had not been for his Uncle George, the house would have been in even worse state. It was he who took over when Miles suddenly bought into the army and left for the Peninsula, and he did what he could to put things to right, but the drawing room was still badly in need of a woman's touch.

It had, however, become a comfortable habit for the two men to get together there for a drink each evening and talk over the events of the day before going in to dinner.

"You'll never believe what I saw this morning, Miles," Sir George said as he sipped a glass of sherry, glad to see his nephew relaxing for a few minutes and forgetting the worries of the estate.

Miles grinned as he stretched himself out comfortably in the large leather wing chair that had been his father's favorite. "I'm sure I'll believe it if you say it was so, George," he rejoined, "but please don't keep me on tenterhooks. What did you see that was so unusual?"

Sir George watched the younger man's face as he told him, "I saw Lady Arabella Barton stepping into Tom Benson's cart carrying a basket, and behind her came Ted Carter, the Summersons' head groom, with a portmanteau and a small hamper."

His nephew looked puzzled. "Do you suppose she was leaving there without the Summersons' knowledge?"

"That's what I did think at first," Sir George said with a nod, "but Ted had seen me, and once the cart had started off down the lane, he waited, appearing anxious to have a word. He's a bright fellow, too good to be wasted on the poor cattle the Summersons keep," he added. "If I hadn't known him to be a stickler for the truth, I'd never have believed him! He told me that they knew she was going, all right, but hadn't lifted so much as a finger to help her."

His expression was one of disgust. "Right now that young widow will be on her way to London by stage, with her cat in that basket and enough food the cook prepared for her, on her own, to last her a couple of days. What she'll do when she gets there, I've no idea, for Tom said she had to get a footman to sell a piece of her jewelry just to pay for the fare.''

Miles sighed in frustration. ''I'd have gladly sent her off in my carriage if she'd have let me, but she's refused to see me each time I've called, and she appeared too embarrassed to linger when I ran into her the other day.''

''That's another thing. It wasn't her who refused to see you, it was old Clarice, and she didn't tell her you'd ever been by until a few days ago. There's not much goes on in that house that the staff there don't know about, and it all filters through to the stables eventually.'' Sir George sounded very pleased with himself.

''Well, there's nothing we can do now, but I hate the thought of her traveling under such conditions.'' Miles sounded completely frustrated. ''Tonight she's probably sleeping in some inn's cold attic on a lumpy mattress on the floor, and sharing with one or more—that's if she's not so short of funds that she goes right through without stopping.''

As Sir George saw the obvious concern on his nephew's face, he realized that Miles was still just as much in love with her as he had been six years ago. He felt the need to reassure the younger man if he could.

''She's not the saucy young chit she used to be, Miles,'' he said. ''And according to Ted Carter, it's not the first time she's traveled by stage, either, for that's the way she arrived here a year ago. If she has to pinch pennies to that extent, she may very well travel right through, and it might be the better option, for the mattress would surely be flea-ridden.

''I agree with you that the Summersons are at fault, but I have a feeling she's learned how to take care of herself since you knew her.'' He frowned, recalling something else. ''One thing I thought strange, though, is that she was careful not to tell any of the servants where she was going in London. Does her father have a house there, for they heard that she hoped to see him?''

Miles smiled a little grimly. He now knew where Arabella would be staying, for he had, by chance, run into her father in London a few years ago and had been invited to dinner with Lord Darnley at his sister's house, where apparently he always stayed when in town. It had been her Aunt Gertrude, the dowager Marchioness of Aylesbury, who was to have brought Arabella out all those years ago, and the good lady had invited Miles to call on her brother there anytime he was in London.

He felt the swift urge to throw some clothes into a bag and start out after her at once, but he would probably not catch up the stage before it reached London now and, in any case, he had responsibilities here that could not be shirked. He also wanted to sleep on it, then make careful plans, for if he did decide to try to win her again, he must be sure of success this time.

The next morning, as he rode out to join his bailiff at one of the small farms, he thought of those years in the army in which he had attained the rank of colonel and had fought under that excellent strategist who was now the Duke of Wellington. It had been unfortunate, to say the least, that after coming through so many battles unscathed, Miles had been badly wounded in one that need never have been fought. The Battle of Toulouse, where Wellington's men had faced Soult once more, was fought in April of 1814, without either side knowing that the war had ended. Napoleon had already abdicated, but word had not reached the south of France in time to stop the slaughter.

The sawbones had wanted to amputate the leg in the field, but Miles was alert enough to stop him from doing so. He had, however, spent the next six months in field hospitals and one in London, before deciding the leg was as good as it was ever going to be despite the constant pain. Perhaps, while in London this time, he'd have a new surgeon, who was making a name for himself, take another look at it.

He smiled a little grimly, but there was a sparkle in his eyes that had been missing for some time. The decision was made, and he was going to London to launch a new campaign, the success of which would still depend upon careful planning and strategy, for he meant to have Arabella for his own this time.

A few hours afterward, when Miles returned to the house

for a late luncheon, Sir George was surprised to see him looking so happy.

"I've made all the necessary arrangements so that I can be away for the next month or two, George," he said with a grin.

His uncle raised his eyebrows. "You're opening up the town house, then? What a jolly good idea!"

It was Miles' turn to look surprised. "I hadn't thought of doing that just for myself," he said. "I'll probably stay in rooms nearby."

"By the time you seek somewhere to stable your horses and house the carriage, you might just as well have the comforts of your own home, surely," Sir George suggested. "In fact, I believe I'll come with you, for I haven't spent a Season in London for many a year and I think I'd rather enjoy it."

Miles tried not to look inhospitable, but when he had made his plans, he had thought of being alone. However, he could hardly refuse George, for he owed him so very much already. When Arabella had gone off with Richard, Miles had thought only of himself when he bought colors in Wellington's army on the Peninsula. Had it not been for George, who had closed his own house down and come here to look after things, the estates his father had left him would have gone to rack and ruin.

He grinned boyishly. "Going to keep an eye on me, George? I've become expert at maneuvers, you know, and you might have difficulty keeping up with me," he warned.

"I'm prepared to take a chance on that, you young rascal," Sir George told him, smiling happily once he realized that Miles did not really mind his presence in town. "Besides, you'll not only need the carriage for evenings, you'll also need your phaeton for cutting a dash about town, and several horses for riding in the park. How could you handle all those and live in rooms?"

"You're right as usual, George, for I hadn't thought of that side of it," Miles admitted, realizing as he helped himself to another slice of the roast and some more peas that he did not remember eating the plate of food Thomas had placed in front of him. His appetite must be improving.

"You mean to succeed this time around, don't you?" Sir George remarked with just a hint of a smile.

"Yes, George, I do. You see, I've never wanted anyone else," Miles admitted bleakly, "so this time I've planned my strategy carefully and I intend to win this campaign. To start with, I'm taking Ben with me, as usual, but not to work directly for me. I'm going to have him apply for a job in Lady Gertrude's stables, so that he can keep an eye on what's going on there."

"You'd do better to have a maid in the house than a man in the stables, Miles, if you're going to spy on her," Sir George advised, pleased with the idea.

Miles gave a short laugh. "I've thought of that, too, but they might suspect a girl from the north. I'm going to use one of the maids at the town house instead—pick the best, of course, and have her apply. They'll be short of help with Arabella arriving suddenly like that, so it will work, you'll see." He paused, frowning. "Don't mistake me, though. I've no wish, nor right, to spy on her. All I'll have them do is let me know what invitations she accepts so that I can make a point of being there also."

"The maid will report to Ben, of course, and he'll report to you," Sir George said, liking the plan more and more. He reached for the wine decanter and poured another glass for each of them. "Let me give you a toast," he said, raising his glass. "Success to the colonel's campaign!"

It was ludicrous, of course, for there was no comparison whatever between the modes of travel, but as Arabella was jostled and bumped in the stagecoach, she could not help but recall that other journey when she had started out to her Aunt Gertrude's six years ago. However, on that occasion, she had never arrived at her destination.

Papa could not go to town yet, for he still had much to do in the north, so Arabella had set out in his comfortable, roomy traveling coach with her abigail, two coachmen, and six outriders. They had reached the inn where they woul spend the first night, and as her abigail was suffering from travel sickness, Arabella had gone down alone to the private parlor reserved in advance for her supper.

When the innkeeper informed her that all the private parlors were full and that a gentleman who claimed to know her was asking if he might share hers, she had refused, of course. Then he had told her that it was Sir Richard Barton. Because he was a friend of Miles', because she had flirted with him a little at some of the parties they had attended, and because she was young and silly enough to think she could take care of herself, she agreed that he could join her.

But where Miles was most circumspect, Richard was not, and he had plied Arabella with wine throughout the meal, and once the servants had left the room, he had dared her to have a glass of brandy with him. Then he had kissed her in a way that no one else had ever done before, and had taken other liberties that had made her head spin and her heart beat so fast that she mistook it for love, which she as yet knew nothing about. The combination of wine, clever hands, and persuasive tongue had done the rest, and before she knew it she was in Richard's phaeton, flying with him through the night, on their way to Gretna Green.

The next morning, when Arabella was feeling sick and had the worst headache she had ever known, Richard had told her that she was completely compromised, no longer a virgin, and that he had left a note at the inn for her father. The carriage would already be on its way back to deliver it to Lord Darnley as quickly as possible. He also told her she should be glad that he was still going to marry her as soon as they crossed the border and that he expected to receive from her father the dowry that had been promised to Miles.

Arabella had often wondered if Richard would have married her if he had not been so confident that he would get the dowry. But they had been married for a week or more when he wrote her father again and found, t̲ ̲s chagrin, that Lord Darnley had cut her off completel̲ ̲ ̲ ̲ ̲ had replied that he no longer had a daughter, ̲ ̲ ̲ ̲ ̲ be a dowry?

Arabella was abruptly brought ba

a sharp elbow made contact with her ribs, and she gasped. The large woman on her right was trying to tear a chunk from a loaf of bread to give to her husband, who was sitting on the opposite side.

The sudden jerk had disturbed Snowball, who started to mew pitifully inside the basket on Arabella's lap, and she murmured softly to quieten him.

"You've got a cat in there, luv, 'ave you?" the fat lady asked, "I 'ope it doesn't want to do summat and make a stink in 'ere."

Arabella could not imagine that anything the cat did could be worse than the stench of unwashed bodies that already pervaded the air in the carriage, but she just smiled faintly and said, "He's traveled before and seems to tolerate it quite well."

The response was a loud sniff from the woman, who then pulled another piece of bread from the loaf, this time with her teeth, and proceeded to chew it while reaching further into the depths of her bag and bringing out two chicken legs. These were immediately grabbed from her clutches by her husband.

"Greedy bugger, aren't you?" she snarled. "I don't know wot this young lady'll think of yer manners."

Her groping hand now produced a piece of chicken breast from the depths, and Arabella tried not to watch as she gnawed at it until there was nothing left except the bones, which she leaned over and tossed out of the carriage window. Then she wiped her mouth on the back of her hand, and her hand on the skirt of her gown.

"Governess, aren't you, miss?" she said to Arabella as though now, having satisfied her hunger, she was ready to make conversation. "I can allus tell 'em by the way they talk fancy like. Just going to a new position, are you, luv? I 'ope they like cats, or ye'll not last long."

"They won't mind, I'm sure," Arabella murmured. "He's very well behaved and stays in my room."

"She's not a governess, you old busybody," her husband sputtered, sending crumbs from his bread flying across the coach. "She's a widderwoman, that's wot she is."

The woman turned as if to question Arabella further, but just then there was the sound of a horn blowing and the coach slowed to enter the courtyard of an inn. The passengers all leapt for the doors trying to be the first ones out, while Arabella sat back and waited.

When the others had alighted, she stepped down and walked in the opposite direction so that she could exercise Snowball on the leash that Ted Carter had made for the purpose. She was glad she had eaten a substantial breakfast, for now she could wait until they stopped again before sampling some of the food Cook had packed.

The next stage of the journey was a little easier, for the heavy woman and her husband must have been going in a different direction and their places had been taken by a middle-aged woman with her young daughter, and Arabella was grateful to have a little more room on the seat.

Snowball, having tasted freedom for a short time, was reluctant to return to the confinement of the basket and made his objections clear by emitting a series of yowls that Arabella tried her best to hush.

"Do you have a kitty in there?" the little girl asked eagerly.

"Now, Barbara, I told you not to speak unless you were spoken to," her mother admonished sternly.

Arabella nodded. "He's three years old already, and should be better behaved," she told the girl.

"Can I have a look?" the child asked, ignoring her mother's forbidding scowl.

"Don't you dare let that cat out in here or I'll call the guard." They were the first words spoken that day by an older woman, gray-haired and tight-lipped, who had been sitting erect in her corner, her back poker-straight, since Arabella first got on the stage.

"I have no intention of opening the lid, ma'am," Arabella told her quietly; then, turning to the child, she said, "If your mama will allow it, you may see him when we stop for supper."

She immediately regretted her offer, for she had hoped at that stop to get a little privacy to eat some of the food Cook had packed, and was already beginning to feel a little faint from the lack of it.

She need not have worried, however, for the child's mother leaned over and slapped the little girl hard across the face, saying, "I said you were not to talk to strangers, and I meant it." Then she turned and glared at Arabella, looking her up and down as if she was not quite respectable.

Arabella sighed, for though she had traveled this way before, her mind had then been filled with thoughts of the duel that had been fought, and with regret at the careless waste of a life, even though she had felt no love for Richard.

For the first time, the woman on Arabella's left spoke to her, and her voice was quiet enough that it could not be heard by the others over the sound of the child's sobs.

"Don't let it upset you, my dear. We're all a little reluctant to trust strangers, for you never know who you might meet on a public stage," the woman said in a voice that was not quite cultured, yet held no hint of its owner's county of birth.

Arabella turned to look at her and saw a woman of some forty or more years, neatly dressed but not fashionably so. The gray eyes held a look of sympathy as the woman remarked, "You're young to be a widow. Was it the war?"

Arabella looked surprised, for she was wearing gloves, of course, over her wedding band, then she noticed that its impression could be seen through the thin leather. "No, it wasn't. My husband died just a year ago," she answered quietly, hoping she would not be questioned further. The cat-hating woman would surely call the guard and have her thrown off the coach if she heard that he had been killed in a duel.

"You could not have been married very long, though, I'm sure, for you don't look much more than twenty years old," the soft, sympathetic voice went on. "At least you're young enough to be able to make a new life for yourself."

It was a relief to speak to someone who was kind, for Arabella had not expected to find a gentlewoman traveling on the stage. She smiled, her face lighting up with pleasure, and she did not notice the interested glint in the other woman's eyes. "I'm just twenty-four," Arabella told her. "I was married when I was eighteen."

"What a nice age to be, my dear, for you have so much of life before you still, and a great deal more to offer than a chit of eighteen," the woman said kindly. "I've been a widow myself for many years. I am Mrs. Gordon, and I am returning to my home in London after a short visit with some friends."

Arabella felt that she should give her own name in return, but was reluctant to give her title. "My name is Arabella Barton, Mrs. Gordon," she said. "I'm very pleased to meet you and happy that you are going all the way to London, as I am, for it is such a tedious journey to travel in silence."

Mrs. Gordon chuckled. "Or to travel with the kind of companions who got off at the last stop, for had they remained they would not have let you alone until they knew everything they could about you. Is it your intention to stop the night at the next inn?"

Arabella shook her head. "I'm going right through, for I can make up the sleep later, and I frankly cannot afford to put out the money for poor accommodations."

Mrs. Gordon nodded understandingly. "That's good, for I had come to the same decision, and we can always doze a little through the night. We'll watch out for each other."

4

Arabella considered herself most fortunate to have met a lady of Mrs. Gordon's quality on a public stage, for the journey was so very much less tedious than it would have been without her quiet, refined conversation. For some reason, Richard had always avoided London, though they had been on the outskirts on more than one occasion. As the stage carried them nearer and nearer, she started to feel like a green girl, for she had not the slightest notion of how to go along when she finally arrived there. How was she going to get from the coaching inn to her aunt's house without money?

"Is this your first visit to London, Arabella?" Mrs. Gordon asked when they started out on the last day of the journey.

"It feels as though it is," Arabella told her frankly, "but my papa did, in fact, bring me here twice before."

Mrs. Gordon nodded. "As a small child, I've no doubt, and he took you to see the menagerie in the Tower, Astley's Circus, or a balloon ascension, and if it was the end of the summer, perhaps to the Bartholomew Fair."

"Probably all of those, but I really don't remember too well," Arabella admitted sheepishly. "It all seemed very exciting at the time, but I saw too much at once and the only thing I remember really clearly is watching the beautiful balloon drift up into the sky so high that the man in the basket beneath it could scarcely be seen from below.''

''And I suppose you wanted to go up with him?'' Mrs. Gordon suggested with amusement.

''Oh, no.'' Arabella was emphatic. ''I had no desire to go up in that contraption, I'm afraid, which surprised my papa very much, for I was usually ready to try anything.''

''An adventurous spirit, I've no doubt,'' the older lady murmured, ''and I'm sure you still retain much of it, or you'd not be in this coach now, hastening to the city. Will there be someone meeting you when we finally get there?''

Arabella shook her head. ''Not this time, for I was not sure of just when I would arrive. I'm going to surprise them,'' she said with a short laugh, hoping her papa would view it as a pleasant one.

For a moment only, Arabella thought she saw a strange expression on her newfound friend's face, and she looked away as a slight shiver of something like fear ran through her. But when she turned to look at Mrs. Gordon once more, she saw only the gentle smile and decided that the loss of sleep must be having an adverse effect upon her.

''We'll be there in less than two hours now,'' Mrs. Gordon said, ''and I, for one, am going to have a sip of brandy and then close my eyes for a while so that I will arrive feeling refreshed. How about you doing the same, my dear Arabella?''

She produced a silver flask from her bag and poured a dark liquid into a silver cup.

''Here, try some, my dear. It's just the thing to pick you up before we get there.'' She held out the cup, but as Arabella reached for it, the coach swerved and the cup and flask both fell to the floor.

As Mrs. Gordon scrambled among people's feet in her efforts to recover her flask, Arabella was sure she heard her use a word that her papa said only under the greatest of stress. She must have been mistaken, she decided, for it would be most odd for such a refined lady to use language of that sort.

"Here," Mrs. Gordon said, holding the flask up in triumph and slipping back into her seat, "let's try again."

But this time, Arabella shook her head. "I think I'd better not, thank you, for I never have had much of a head for spirits," she said firmly.

"Just as you wish," Mrs. Gordon said abruptly, shrugging slightly as she replaced the flask and cup in her handbag without taking some of it for herself.

Arabella had not much time to think about this, however, for the coach swerved again and suddenly appeared to be traveling at a most dangerous speed.

"We must have picked up one of those young men who fancy themselves whips and pay the coachman to let them drive," Mrs. Gordon whispered. "You'd best say your prayers that we don't turn over."

Swaying unsteadily from side to side, the coach raced through the narrow streets, while all of the passengers clung to their seats and peered anxiously out the windows. Arabella could not help but pity the poor people who were riding on top, for it seemed that they might quite easily be thrown completely off. She breathed a sigh of relief when one last swerve put them in the courtyard of the large inn that was their final destination.

This time Arabella did not wait for the others to get out first, for she suddenly felt an urgent desire to find her bag and get away from the coach as quickly as possible. As she stepped down, she could not help but notice a private coach and driver waiting nearby. There was also a hackney with a burly young coachman standing by the side of it, and she wondered if he might be persuaded to take her to her aunt's house if she promised that her aunt would pay him when they got there.

A guard was throwing the bags down from the top, and just as Arabella saw hers land almost at her feet, she felt Mrs. Gordon's hand on her arm, grasping her sleeve. "I have a carriage waiting, my dear. Come, I'll send my coachman to get your bag and then we'll see you safely home."

There was sudden confusion as others searched for their

baggage, and Snowball's pitiful mewing only made things worse. Mrs. Gordon's hold on Arabella's sleeve had tightened and she was determinedly pulling her away from the bag she was trying to reach. Suddenly the big hackney driver took a hold of Arabella's other arm and she thought for a moment that she might be torn in half.

"Let go, Mother Gordon," the big man's deep voice commanded. "This is one innocent ye're not getting."

Almost effortlessly, he scooped up Arabella's large bag and slammed it against Mrs. Gordon's side, forcing her to release her hold, and then, half-carrying and half-pulling, he drew Arabella across to his hackney.

"Now, young lady," he said, still holding her firmly by the arm, "tell me where ye planned to spend t'night, an' I'll take ye there myself."

The man was shabbily dressed, and he was far from handsome, but he had the sincerest brown eyes she could ever recall seeing.

"I have no money, but—" she began.

"If ye've somewhere t'go to, I'll take ye there," he said gruffly, "and if ye don't know anywhere safe where ye can spend the night, I know of a place where ye'll come to no 'arm."

"Thank you, sir, but my aunt is expecting me, and I know she'll pay your fare," Arabella said, "if you'll take me there."

Without a word, he handed her into the cab, put her bag and Snowball beside her, and got onto the driver's seat. "Now give me t'address," he said.

"It's Hanover Square, Number Eighteen," she told him, and saw the big man's eyebrows lift in surprise. She gave him a rather tremulous smile, adding, "It's true, my aunt is Lady Fitzwilliam."

They started out, and once they were clear of the inn yard, he told her to lean forward. "There are some things I want to say to ye afore we get there, and I don't want to 'ave to keep turning around."

Arabelle dutifully leaned forward.

"For a niece of a fine lady, ye're a mite slow," he said

in an exasperated voice. " 'Ave ye any idea what ye almost got yerself into with Mother Gordon?''

"But she didn't seem like that until . . . until we were quite close to London," she protested.

"Like what?'' he asked. "Like t'proprietress of an 'igh-class brothel?''

Arabella gasped and swallowed hard. "I think I'm going to be sick,'' she muttered.

"Not in my cab, ye're not,'' he snapped. "Just pull yerself together, and someday ye'll be able to tell yer children wot almost 'appened to ye.''

"Are you sure that's what she is?'' Arabella had to ask again, for it seemed quite incongruous.

"She gets 'er young ladies by ridin' up an' down on t'stage, and lookin' for likely 'uns,'' he grunted. "Did she share a room with you at the inn last night?''

"No,'' Arabella said emphatically. "I told her I was riding right through on the stage, and it seemed that she was also.''

His chuckle ended in a coughing bout. When he was over it, he said, "That's a good one. Mother Gordon 'avin' to sit up all night on t'stage and then losin' 'er quarry to me.'' They had reached Hanover Square, and he slowed the horse to a walk and peered at the houses until he saw Number Eighteen. "I'll go ring t'bell and then come back for ye,'' he told her.

He was remarkably spry for a man of his size. He had already clanged the doorbell loudly, had helped Arabella out of the cab, and had placed her cat, still in the basket, into her arms before the door opened. Dawson, Lady Gertrude's butler, stood in the entrance, an expression of astonishment on his usually impassive face.

"Good evening,'' Arabella said with as much poise as she could muster. "I'm Lady Arabella Barton . . .''

There was a cry of surprise, and suddenly a tall, slender lady came flying out of the house. Quite obviously in her middle years, she was elegantly gowned in a shade of blue to match her eyes, and not a single blond curl dared to slip out of place as she gathered Arabella into her arms.

"My dear, we were so worried about you, for you didn't

tell us how you were going to get here, or when," she scolded, "and if you had arrived just two minutes later, you would have missed me."

Over Arabella's shoulder she saw the cabdriver standing watching them with a look of amusement on his face.

"You came by hackney, my dear? From where?" she asked a little hesitantly.

"From the Bell and Bottle coaching inn, ma'am, an' you must be Lady Fitzwilliam," the gruff voice was not disrespectful, but neither was it servile. "If she woz my niece, I'd make 'er so sore she'd never want to travel alone by stage again." He touched his cap. "Now I know she's safe, I'll be gettin' along."

"You come right back here," Arabella called after him. "He's not yet been paid, Auntie, for I have no money."

Dawson reached into his pocket and walked over to the cabdriver, handing him some coins, but before he had completed the task, Lady Fitzwilliam joined them, took a golden guinea from the coins in Dawson's palm, and dropped it into that of the cabdriver.

"I've a feeling we owe you a great deal more than that, young man," she said sternly. "If I can ever be of service to you, please let me know."

Turning back to Arabella, she steered her into the house and through to the drawing room. "It's a pity your papa is out to dinner tonight," she said, frowning, "or, then again, perhaps it's not, for I think you and I are a little overdue a nice, long cose. You look a bit pinched. Did you not have luncheon?"

When her niece shook her head, Lady Gertrude went over to the bellpull and gave it a sharp tug, then sat down at a small inlaid mahogany desk and started to write a brief note.

Arabella took a seat on a small settee and waited. It seemed almost too good to be true that she was really here at last, with this warm, kind aunt she could trust and tell everything to—or almost everything. She did not know yet if her father would even speak to her, let alone forgive her, but she loved him very much and knew she must try very hard for a reconciliation.

"Dawson, please have someone take this to Lady Berkeley's home right away, and there is no need to wait for a reply," Lady Fitzwilliam instructed as she gave him the note. "And tell Cook that there has been a change of plan. I would like a light supper served in the dining room in forty-five minutes for Lady Arabella and myself, and you may serve sherry here in fifteen minutes."

As the butler departed, she turned to her niece. "Now, my dear, let me show you to the bedchamber that has already been prepared for you, for I'm so excited at the thought of you and my brother becoming reconciled at last that I just can't stop talking. He's missed you terribly, you know, and looks much more than six years older than when you last saw him."

"I've missed him, too," Arabella said sadly. "I didn't blame him at all for not sending my dowry to Richard, but when he wrote that he no longer had a daughter . . . " She broke off, too close to tears to continue.

"He didn't mean that, I can assure you, my love," Lady Fitzwilliam said firmly, leading the way along the corridor. "He has been worrying about you every bit as much as I have these last few days, wondering if you had been kidnapped, or worse, on the road."

Arabella could not repress a teary chuckle. "I'll tell you all about it just as soon as I come down," she said, giving her aunt a warm hug; then she entered the bedchamber, closed the door, and released Snowball from the confining basket.

It seemed he had also been expected, for his needs had been provided for and bowls of food and water set out in the adjoining maid's room.

It was a delightful bedchamber, with a big four-poster bed hung with a cabbage rose patterned fabric and a dainty dressing table, chair, and armoire of a light cherry wood. Two comfortable chairs, covered in the rose fabric, were placed in front of the fireplace, and there was even an inlaid escritoire beneath the window for her use.

A jug on the dressing table contained water with rose petals floating on top, and Arabella poured some of it into the bowl and washed the grime of the road from her hands and face; then, admonishing Snowball to be on his best behavior, she hurried downstairs to join her aunt.

"Now, you simply must tell me what happened on your journey," Lady Fitzwilliam insisted, "for from what that rather outspoken hackney driver said, I suspect you must have put yourself in some kind of danger."

A sip of the excellent sherry gave Arabella the courage she needed to begin. "I came by stage, as you no doubt realized, and it seemed I was most unfortunate with my traveling companions from the start," she explained. "They were quite rude, but then a lady sitting quietly to my left saw that I was somewhat upset, and started a friendly conversation, which continued until we reached London."

"Well, although I've never in my life journeyed by stage, I am glad to know that there are some nice people who travel that way," Lady Fitzwilliam declared, "but I have a feeling there is much more to be told."

"Just before we reached London, she tried to persuade me to drink something out of a flask she was carrying, and I might very well have done so had it not fallen to the floor when the carriage swerved." Arabella's eyes were twinkling as she described what had happened when the stagecoach reached its destination, but Lady Fitzwilliam was quite shocked. Her hand shook as she reached for the sherry decanter and helped herself to another glass.

"What a dreadful woman! I think we'd best not tell your papa, my dear," she advised, "or he will not want to let you out of his sight for fear it might happen again."

Arabella agreed. "I have no wish to worry him unnecessarily," she said, "and would not have told you anything about it had not the cabdriver already made you suspicious. He was very good to me, but made me feel like a silly schoolgirl instead of a twenty-four-year-old widow."

There was the sound of a discreet cough from the door, then Dawson announced, "Dinner is served, my lady," and led the way to the formal dining room, where two places were set at one end of the large table.

With more servants in attendance than diners, conversation

was necessarily limited until they had finished several courses, the sweet had been put before them, and a tea tray placed on the table, at which point Aunt Gertrude smilingly dismissed the staff.

Arabella concealed a giggle behind her napkin, for she had forgotten that her aunt was the Dowager Marchioness of Aylesford and lived in the style to which she had become accustomed when she married the marquess many years ago. She recalled her father telling her once that his sister had paid so dearly for her title that she never wished to marry again, but Arabella was uncertain at that time as to how her aunt had "paid." After her own five-year marriage she could now hazard a guess, but could not, of course, be sure.

"After sleeping the last few nights in a moving carriage, I am sure that you will be eager to get to bed tonight," Lady Fitzwilliam said sympathetically, "and I really do not know when your papa might return. However, perhaps we can decide first what we will do in the morning. Am I safe in assuming from that one bag that your wardrobe is much depleted?"

"Quite safe, Aunt Gertrude," Arabella said dryly. "I have two more gowns similar to this one, and that is all, for I had no wish to keep the kind of gowns Richard bought for me to wear. But though I will be happy to come out of black gloves, I will not need much, for I cannot, of course, take part in social activities."

Her aunt's eyebrows rose. "Pray tell me your reasoning behind such a ridiculous remark, my dear," she requested, "for I find it difficult to believe that you are serious."

"You cannot have forgotten that my husband's death in a duel was the talk of last Season, for my sister-in-law received a great many letters from so-called friends, telling her it was so scandalous it would never be lived down," Arabella responded in a hurt tone.

The marchioness smiled kindly. "My dear, there are so many things happening all the time here that one scandal fades as quickly as the next one comes along, and is completely forgotten in a month. I promise you that few people will remember it, and fewer still will have ever heard of your former indiscretion when you eloped with Richard six years ago.

"At first it was thought that you had been the cause of the duel, and I must admit that would have made things a little difficult for you, but when word came that it had been fought over card play, you were completely exonerated, of course," she added, with a satisfied nod.

But not by everyone, Arabella could not help but think, for there must be at least one person who thought her at fault and was sending those dreadful notes. Perhaps, now she was in London, she would be safe from him.

The front doorbell sounded, and a few moments later Lord Darnley entered the dining room, closed the door behind him, and stood for a moment gazing at his only child. Tears sprang to Arabella's eyes as she saw the new lines in his face and the white hair that had once been the color of her own. He beckoned, and she rose and walked slowly forward, halting a few feet from him before flinging herself into his outstretched arms. Neither of them noticed when Lady Fitzwilliam quietly slipped out of the room.

It was almost a half-hour before they joined her in the drawing room. Lord Darnley's voice appeared somewhat huskier than usual, and Arabella's eyes were puffed with weeping, but they both looked extremely happy to be together once more.

Lady Fitzwilliam handed a cup of tea to her niece and placed the decanter of port by the side of her brother, then resumed her seat on the sofa. She looked quite pleased with herself as she told Lord Darnley, "When you interrupted us, Kenneth, we were discussing Arabella's need for a complete new wardrobe of clothes, for she has nothing at all save for those dismal widow's weeds. She was trying to convince me earlier that she needs little in the way of gowns because the nature of Richard's death puts her beyond the pale."

"As my daughter, Arabella will be accepted everywhere," he growled, "and she will, of course, be presented at court as soon as possible."

"And as my niece, Kenneth, she will most certainly receive invitations from everyone of any consequence, and she must be outfitted at once in the very latest styles," Lady Fitzwilliam pronounced. "I believe she is a trifle short of funds, however, so I will pay—"

"You will send all the bills to me," Lord Darnley broke in sternly. "And don't stint, for I won't have anyone saying that I've become clutch-fisted in my old age."

Arabella stared at the two of them trying to outdo each other in attending to her best interests, and she felt a little overwhelmed. She had counted her pennies for too many years to now spend money carelessly, and she vowed to put a curb on her aunt when she went with her to the modiste. She was not in the marriage market any longer and she did not intend to go to any functions her aunt would not normally attend.

She listened to the two of them happily bickering about where she was to go and whom they would invite first to meet her, and the unhappy year she had spent with the Summersons seemed to fade as though it had ended a long time ago instead of just a few days.

All at once, she felt very tired, as though even the effort to rise from the chair would be too much, and a few minutes later her aunt noticed the problem she was having in just keeping her eyes open.

"Come along, my dear," Lady Fitzwilliam said, slipping an arm around her niece. "I think it's time for us to leave your papa to his port. Try to get a good night's sleep, for first thing in the morning you and I are going shopping. It will be such fun! Just like having a daughter of my own to outfit for the Season."

Arabella was asleep before her head had scarcely touched the pillow, and though she had been afraid that she might be disturbed by nightmares about her journey, the events of the day did not disturb her in the least. Instead, she awoke the next morning from an interesting dream in which Miles Cavendish played a most prominent part, for his arms were around her and she could actually feel the warm touch of

his lips on her own. They were gently demanding, not rough
as Richard's had been, and a silky finger was gently stroking
her cheek.

A smile still lingered on her face as she opened her eyes
to gaze directly into those of Snowball. A small paw touched
her cheek, then he let out a plaintiff meow, jumped down
from the bed, and went over to the door to the maid's room,
which must have been closed all night.

She got quickly out of bed and took care of his problem;
then, stretching lazily, she stood looking out of the window
at the trees in the square: they were just starting to burst into
leaf, a harbinger of spring and a new beginning for her also.

5

It seemed to Arabella that her aunt employed an enormous number of servants to look after so few people, for she had no sooner slipped into a dressing gown than a maid knocked and entered carrying a cup of hot chocolate.

Then, not ten minutes later, another maid came in with a steaming jug of water that she set down on the dressing table and took away the one from last night.

All that remained after that was for yet another rather shy girl to enter, this time a little younger than Arabella; she smiled sweetly and told her she was to be milady's personal maid for now.

Arabella had not had an abigail since she had lived at home with her papa, and so she now appreciated all the more the luxury of being able to sit down and have someone else try to tame her unruly hair.

"What did you say your name was?" Arabella asked as she peered in the mirror, noting that the girl's work was little better than her own efforts.

"Peg, my lady," the girl told her, then went over to the armoire and took out one of the black dresses.

"Well, Peg, you are certainly gentle with the brush," Arabella said kindly, for the girl did not appear to have quite the right touch with her hair. "Now, if you could turn that black dress into a fashionable green walking gown, you would really be a miracle worker."

Peg smiled, holding the gown out in front of her. "It's not quite the latest style, my lady," she admitted, "but no doubt you've come to town early to order new gowns."

Arabella nodded. "My aunt and I are to go shopping this morning, I believe, so there will soon be clothes more elegant than this old thing to take care of. How glad I shall be to wear colors for a change," she remarked as she stepped into the gown and waited until it was completely fastened. "I hope my aunt is not already at breakfast, for I'm hungry but would not like to keep her waiting."

"I don't believe her ladyship has left her bedchamber yet," Peg murmured, "so you will have plenty of time, milady."

With a smile of thanks, Arabella hurried down the stairs and had already heaped her plate with a considerable portion of food before her aunt came into the room.

"That's the way, my dear." Lady Fitzwilliam looked very pleased with her niece's appetite. "You'll need to be well fortified before we start out, for we've much work ahead of us if we are to get you done up in style. We'll start with my modiste, Madame Dubois, and see if she has anything that can be altered for you to wear at once, and of course, we'll order the rest of the gowns. Then we'll take swatches of fabric with us and visit the glovemaker, the milliner, and the shoemaker. If we have time, we'll also go to the haberdasher and the draper, but that depends on how many people are already in town and doing the same thing as we are."

"I feel quite guilty," Arabella declared. "I'm sure there must be a great many things you would rather do this morning than spend the entire time having me fitted with clothes."

Lady Fitzwilliam chuckled. "Do you know, my dear," she confided, "I've always regretted not having a daughter of my own that I could bring out, and had been so looking forward to sponsoring you, helping with your clothes, giving parties, and so forth. But then you let me down terribly by running off with that young man. Now, it seems, I've been given a second chance, and I intend to enjoy every minute of it.''

Impulsively, Arabella leaned over and kissed her aunt's cheek. "I wish we had been closer when I was younger, for with your guidance I might not have made such a foolish mistake as to marry Richard," she said ruefully. "But then you had the marquess to look after, I'm sure."

Her aunt grunted. "We'd best not start talking about him or we'll be at the breakfast table all day," Lady Fitzwilliam said dryly. "As you know, many widows have little cause to regret their new status and many good reasons for not remarrying."

Although Arabella would have liked to have seen her father for a moment before they left, her aunt appeared eager to be off and had ordered the carriage already, so the two of them set off immediately after breakfast for Madame Dubois' establishment.

Three hours later, Arabella could fully understand why her aunt had been so anxious to make an early start. It was a completely different experience from anything she had known in the north of England, for there the dressmaker was sent for and she stayed at the house making gowns and other garments according to the wishes of the lady of the house.

Madame Dubois was, however, a law unto herself, for it was she who decided what fabric and style best suited her customer, and even the outspoken Lady Fitzwilliam did not give the Frenchwoman any argument.

Arabella had to admit that the woman had excellent taste and had an exceptional eye for color. However, when she tried on a gown that was already made and saw how low a neckline was intended, she made her objections loud and clear.

"But, my lady," Madame Dubois said airily, "you can always put a little fichu here until you become accustomed to it; I assure you that all the ladies of the *ton* will be wearing the low line this Season, for it is the latest fashion from Paris."

Arabella was adamant, however. "I have worn fichus for five years and am now weary of them. I want the necklines of all my gowns to be cut no lower than this." She pointed to the desired place and warned, "If they are any lower, I will not accept the gowns."

Madame Dubois shrugged, then spoke to her assistant in rapid French. "It shall be as you wish, my lady, but I'm sure that before the Season is out, you'll be asking me to make them lower for you," she said confidently.

The two ladies were quite relieved to be offered coffee and French pastries, for they had been there for more than two hours, and Arabella had still to try on other already-made clothes, to be altered for her immediate use.

"I assume that Richard had a low taste in necklines," Lady Fitzwilliam said as she sipped the delicious French coffee. "I'm surprised, however, for husbands usually like to see them only on other women."

Arabella smiled at her aunt, realizing how little she knew of the life she had lived with Richard. Perhaps it was time she told her something of it.

"The low necklines were intended to put off his opponents in the card games he constantly played," she explained, "and he would buy and present me with the gowns I was to wear. However, as I said, I became accustomed to covering myself with fichus, scarves, and wraps, for I grew to strongly dislike seeing men ogling me."

"I'm not at all surprised, for it's quite disgusting, to say the least," the older woman murmured. "Couldn't you have developed a megrim and stayed in your room?"

Arabella's eyes were hard and her smile fixed as she said quietly, "When I tried to do so, he always made certain that my indisposition was not just an excuse—and I still had to put in an appearance at the tables."

They returned to Hanover Square a little after two in the afternoon, and both ladies immediately retired to their rooms for an hour or two. Visits to a number of small shops to buy hats, gloves, shoes, and such, after leaving the modiste, had left them both completely exhausted.

By retiring, however, they completely missed the visit Lord Darnley received from Lord Cavendish.

Miles had sent a note around a little earlier, asking if he

might call on Arabella's father, and the latter had readily agreed, though wondering why Cavendish should wish to see him. Lord Darnley had been aware, of course, that the young man had returned from the war quite badly wounded. He had, in fact, seen him a couple of times in London and had him here to dinner once, but no mention had been made of Arabella, for she was obviously not a subject either man wished to bring up.

He was a little surprised that Cavendish had not suggested meeting at his club, and concluded that it must be a personal rather than a business matter he wished to speak to him about.

Cavendish came at four o'clock, when the ladies were having tea in their bedchambers, and Lord Darnley ordered brandy to be served in the study. He looked up as the younger man limped into the room, and would have risen had he not felt it might serve to emphasize the other's disability. Instead, he smiled and motioned to a comfortable chair by the side of the desk.

"It's good to see you again, my boy," Lord Darnley said warmly. "I was unaware that you were in town or I would have suggested dinner at my club."

Miles smiled somewhat apologetically. "I'm afraid I'm rushing my fences, sir, as my father would have said, but I wanted to make sure as soon as possible that I had not come on a fool's errand." He chuckled softly. "Uncle George came with me, and we only arrived this morning, so I was glad to leave him to take care of all the things he insists must be done for our comfort."

"You plan a lengthy stay, then?" Lord Darnley asked in some surprise. "You don't usually come for the Season, do you?"

Miles shook his head. "Haven't done so in years, but then there's so much to do on the estates that it leaves little time for frivolities."

Lord Darnley leaned forward. "You should do as I do, Miles. I hired a first-class man to take care of everything, then I just go back and check on him thoroughly every six months or so. It costs a bit more than if I did it myself, but, you see"—he gave a helpless shrug and a sadness came into his eyes then quickly disappeared—"I just hadn't the heart to keep up to everything when there was no one I cared to leave it to. But now things are different and I shall be making a few changes."

The younger man nodded. "Yes, things are different, sir," he said, "and that's just what I came to talk to you about."

A look of surprise came over Lord Darnley's face and he reached for the decanter of brandy. "Is it, now?" he remarked, pouring a generous portion into each glass and handing one to Miles. "Then you know that my daughter and I are reconciled at last?"

"I know that she came to London, sir," Miles said quietly, "and it was my hope that the two of you could forget the past, for she needs you at this time every bit as much as you need her."

"She's not the same flighty miss as you were courting, Miles," Lord Darnley told him. "She hasn't talked about it yet to me, but she must have had a hard time with Barton. Do you know that she came here on the stagecoach, alone without even the money for a hackney from the coaching inn?"

"I would have gladly sent her in my carriage, sir, but I was unaware that she was leaving until George told me she'd already left—in Tom Benson's cart, and the Summersons knew about it," Miles said bitterly.

"My girl's still got spirit, despite five years with that no-good bastard." Lord Darnley was too angry for words.

"I do not think his parentage was in question, sir," Miles said with a grim smile, "but his morals were a completely different matter. I have to take some of the blame, for I introduced him to her and trusted him completely."

Lord Darnley looked at the young man as he sat with his stiff leg stretched out in front of him. He was still a fine figure of a man, as handsome as ever, though pain had etched a few lines on his face. There had never been any question in his mind that Cavendish was right for Arabella, but was she right for him after what she had been through? That was the question, and one this young man would have to find out for himself.

"So, you still want her after what she did to you." It was a statement rather than a question, and Lord Darnley could not hide the small gleam of satisfaction in his eyes. "She might not be able to give you heirs, for she had no children in the five years she was wed to Barton," he warned.

Miles smiled broadly. "Not only do I still want her, sir, but I mean to have her this time," he said firmly. "And I'm willing to take my chance as to whether she is barren or not. For all we know, Barton could have been impotent or sterile. What I want from you is your approval of my courtship."

"And my encouragement, of course. I'll be sure she knows what a good prospect you still are," Lord Darnley said with a grin.

But Miles shook his head firmly. "No, sir," he said emphatically. "I don't want her to even know I am courting her, and I'm counting on you to keep quiet about the purpose of my visit today. She and I were friends once. I want her to feel that way again, if possible, and then go from there."

Lord Darnley poured another glass of brandy for them. "We'll have a toast, then. To your success, my boy, for I can't think of anyone I'd rather have for a son-in-law." They both drank to it, then Lord Darnley said, "I'll have my man draw up the dowry agreement, and as it's been invested for six more years, it's gained quite a bit since last time."

"I don't need it," Miles declared, "and I'll probably have you put it into her name, start a trust that can pass only from mother to daughter, perhaps. Ask your man about it. I know it can be done."

Lord Darnley's eyebrows had risen at Miles' words. "I hope my daughter realizes how very fortunate she is. Very few of us get a second chance, and she cost you so much." He looked at the injured leg as he spoke.

Miles shook his head. "No, I did that, not Arabella. I enjoyed my service under Wellington, sir, and it taught me a great deal. I trust you to be sure that neither she nor Lady Fitzwilliam have any idea that I mean to marry her, when she also is willing, for I would rather they think of me as just an old friend from the country for now."

"Then you're lucky I did not tell them I expected you,"

Lord Darnley said, "for it was pure chance that they happened to be out all morning shopping and retired to rest as soon as they got back."

"I'm sure I was, sir," Miles said with a grin as he shook hands with the older man. And I intend to continue to be lucky, he thought as the butler handed him his hat and gloves, for he had sent Ben and Dora to this house earlier in the day to apply for positions, and they had both been successful. They were to start in their new posts first thing tomorrow.

The two ladies were sipping a sherry before dinner when Lord Darnley came into the drawing room. His meeting with Miles Cavendish had put him into the happiest frame of mind, and he positively beamed at his sister. To his surprise, she did not return his smile.

"I'm glad someone is happy in this house," Lady Fitz-william said sharply. "Can you believe that after spending half the day getting Arabella outfitted for the Season—and tiring ourselves so much that we both had to retire to our chambers at once—she refuses to accompany me this evening to a card party one of my very dear friends is giving."

Lord Darnley looked from one to the other of them, still smiling happily. "Is this one of your new gowns?" he asked his daughter.

"Yes, it is," his sister snapped, "and Madame Dubois had it altered and sent around late this afternoon just so that Arabella could go out this evening."

"Are you tired, my dear?" Lord Darnley asked Arabella. "I've never indulged in the occupation, but have been told that shopping is one of the most tiring of practices."

"No, Papa," Arabella told him. "I'm not at all tired, but I don't wish to go out this evening until I know whether or not you are staying at home. If you are, I'd like nothing better than to spend the evening here with you, for we've not yet had a chance to really talk since I arrived."

"Why on earth didn't you tell me?" her aunt began. "If that's the case, I could have—"

"You could have told her that indeed I had planned to have a quiet night at home for once," Lord Darnley interrupted firmly, "but I did not realize a gown would be ready so quickly. I would like nothing better, my pet, than for you and me to spend the evening catching up a little on the last six years. Gertrude can go to her card party alone, as she intended to do when she accepted the invitation."

The look in his daughter's eyes more than made up for the loss of an evening's card play at his club. They really did need to get to know each other again. He had not changed, of course, but Arabella had been through a lot, and she not only looked different but behaved with much more consideration than she had ever done before.

Lady Fitzwilliam was all smiles again. "I could have told her nothing of the sort, Kenneth, for you had not divulged your plans for the evening. Nor had your daughter said what she wanted to do instead of accompanying me. Of course you must spend the evening together, and as many other evenings as you wish, for it's been far too long since you were able to do so."

There was a discreet cough and then Dawson announced that dinner was served, and the three of them went into the dining room, a lady on each of Lord Darnley's arms.

As soon as they were finished, Lady Fitzwilliam excused herself, and Arabella elected to have her tea tray brought into the dining room so that she could stay there with her father while he smoked a cigar and had a glass of port.

"It's been a long time, my pet, hasn't it?" Lord Darnley said, taking one of her small hands and holding it in his.

"Too long," Arabella whispered, close to tears but determined not to be a watering pot, "but I never blamed you at all for refusing to give Richard the dowry. He didn't deserve it, and neither did I for what I had done to you."

"What made you do it, my dear?" He was now able to ask her the question that he had asked himself so many times over the years. "I had no idea you knew Barton so well."

"I didn't know him well at all," she admitted, "but when he arrived at the inn where you had told us to spend the night, and the innkeeper said there were no more private parlors available, I was too young and silly to realize that it was all part of a plan he'd conceived."

Lord Darnley looked shocked. "And here I've been thinking all these years that you had never intended to go to London but had planned the whole thing," he said bitterly. "But surely he could do nothing when you had your abigail with you?"

"She turned out to be a real ninnyhammer, Papa. She became travel sick and was too ill, when we got to the inn, to come down to dinner, so I went down alone," Arabella admitted, a little shamefaced. "If it happened now, I would have food sent up to my bedchamber, but I was terribly headstrong in those days, as you well know."

"So he paid the abigail to tell him where you would be spending the night, and told her to be too sick to come down to dinner," he said with a grunt of disgust. "And he gave you wine, which you never did have a head for, so then it was easy for him to do whatever he wanted with you."

Arabella looked at her father with a surprised expression on her face. "Do you know that in all these years I never realized that he must have paid off that abigail. I thought he'd spoken to the coachman, or something," she said. "He didn't do anything to me that night, though he told me the next morning that he had, and I didn't know he was lying, for apparently I passed out from the wine and brandy."

"It wouldn't have made much difference, for you were completely compromised once you'd spent the night with him," Lord Darnley said sadly. "The blackguard deliberately set out to steal you from his friend, and in his note he led me to believe that you were a party to the whole thing. The bullet was too quick a death for the likes of him."

"It's over now, Papa," Arabella said softly. "Richard was to blame, but so was I, for he could not have got away with it had I been a more ladylike, biddable young woman."

Lord Darnley shook his head. "Oh, yes, he would. A man of that sort, determined to get you at all costs, would have kidnapped you if all else had failed. I, too, was at fault, if you like, for sending you to London alone like that. I should have made you wait until I could escort you myself."

Arabella put out a hand and gently stroked his cheek, tender love for him shining in her eyes. "You were too good to me, Papa. I was headstrong and you couldn't say no to me. A sound whipping would have done me good, but I was all you had and you would never have raised a finger to me."

"He didn't beat you, did he?" he demanded to know, suddenly realizing the possibility.

She shrugged. "Sometimes he did, when he lost and blamed me for not distracting his opponents the way he wished me to. You don't imagine that your recalcitrant daughter calmly agreed to do everything he wanted her to, do you?"

Suddenly he thought about his meeting with Miles that afternoon. "I don't suppose he left you alone, yet you had no children in five years of marriage. Was it his fault, do you think?"

"Yes, in a way. There were things he told me to do to prevent having children, for the last thing he wished to be saddled with were some screaming brats, as he put it." She shrugged. "And I certainly didn't want to bear his children."

"Would you marry again if you got the opportunity?" he asked. "You're still a young and beautiful woman."

"Are you trying to get rid of me so soon, Papa?" Arabella asked with a chuckle, for she did not wish to talk seriously about that subject.

"Of course I'm not," Lord Darnley declared, putting an arm around her shoulders. "I've got my little girl back at last, and as far as I am concerned, she can stay with me forever if she wishes to. I just wondered if you'd come to London to find yourself a husband."

Arabella shook her head. "No more than Aunt Gertrude has," she said, "for I'm sure she's never regretted her widowed state. After spending a year with Richard's sister, Clarice, constantly telling me what a wonderful husband Richard was and how I'd never find anyone willing to wed someone as useless as I am, I just want a quiet, peaceful life for a while."

"Well, it's not going to be too peaceful staying with Gertrude, for I know she is already planning a party to introduce you to everyone, and you saw how disappointed she was tonight when you were not going to the card party with her," Lord Darnley warned. "Just don't decide you're through with men because of a cad like Richard, that's all I ask, my dear."

Arabella rose and gestured her papa not to get up. "I'm going to bed now, for I find myself not yet completely rested from the journey. I'm not bitter, Papa, but neither am I eager to marry again. But Richard was very different, and I won't judge others by him, I promise."

He did rise and give her a big hug before releasing her and watching her light step as she walked across the room. At the door she blew him a kiss before going into the hall.

As he resumed his seat and poured himself another glass of port, he realized that, despite his conversation with Miles, he was not eager, either, for her to marry again just yet.

6

Arabella was sitting up in bed, drinking hot chocolate and trying to recall her conversation last night with her papa. When she had finally left him, to catch up on her missed sleep, she had been exceedingly tired, but nonetheless pleased, for he had been so happy that he even looked younger than he had when she first arrived. She could not quite decide, however, from the questions he had posed, whether he wanted her to marry again or did not want her to marry again.

But it was of little importance at the moment, for until she was sure that the person sending her the anonymous threatening letters was no longer able to find her, she could not consider entering into a close relationship with anyone. Besides, the only man she had ever really liked would certainly not marry her now after what she had done to him.

There was a knock on the door and a maid came in with a letter in hand. Arabella bit her lip to stop herself shouting to the girl to take it away, for she suddenly knew what it was. It seemed as if just thinking about the writer of those dreadful notes had caused another one to appear.

"This came for you, my lady, but nobody seems to know when. It wasn't there last night when Mr. Dawson locked

up, but he found it on the hall table first thing this morning."
The girl gave a little bob and put the letter into Arabella's
hands.

Arabella resisted the urge to throw the letter back at the
maid and, instead, quietly thanked her while placing it on
the counterpane as though its contents were of no
consequence to her. But when the girl was almost at the door,
Arabella called, "Please tell Peg not to come up until I ring."

It was a good thing she had remembered to do that, she
thought, for she must open the letter and did not want
inquisitive eyes seeing her tremble as she had when she first
read the others.

She slipped out of bed and went over to the escritoire, then
reached for the letter opener and slid it under the seal. Slowly,
she unfolded the piece of paper and spread it out before her.

The unmistakable large block letters seemed to jump
toward her: "I TOLD YOU HIDING WAS NO GOOD. I AM YOUR
SHADOW AND YOUR CONSCIENCE. LOOK BEHIND YOU."

The page dropped from Arabella's trembling hands, and
she sat staring at it for a few minutes, then she picked it up,
reached for her writing case, and pushed it hurriedly into
the back behind the others.

She did not hear the first knock on the door, and when
the second one sounded, she was so startled that she could
not find her voice. She watched the door opening and held
her breath, but released it when Aunt Gertrude breezed in,
stopping when she saw the empty bed.

Arabella must have made a sound, for her aunt swung
around.

"There you are, my dear," Lady Fitzwilliam said, striding
over and embracing her niece warmly. "You're rested, I
hope, after such a nice long sleep?"

Arabella nodded, still unable to talk, but her aunt did not
notice as she went on, "I have been going to mention something to you about your hair, for that girl that I sent you was
just not adept enough for my liking. By a lucky chance, one
of the new maids we hired for the Season has had some
experience, and I'm giving you her instead." She turned

toward the door and called, "Come along in, Dora, and meet your new mistress."

Arabella liked the smiling girl at once, for she was not forward, nor yet frightened. Lady Fitzwilliam departed, leaving Arabella in the new maid's hands, and in an amazingly short time she was dressed and ready to go down to breakfast. When Arabella saw how well her hair looked, she breathed a sigh of relief, for there was no doubt that the girl had talent.

"Do you like it, my lady?" Dora asked with a smile, passing her a mirror so that she could see the back.

"It's perfect," Arabella told the maid, "and what's more, it feels very safe, not as though it is going to fall down at any moment. You must have worked as a lady's maid before."

Dora nodded. "Yes, my lady, I have, but when I first came to London, it being out of Season, I could only find general maid work."

"And, where you were employed, were there no ladies coming to stay for the Season who might have needed your help?" Arabella asked curiously.

"No, my lady," Dora told her truthfully. "It was a bachelor establishment and two gentlemen just arrived for a few months."

"Well, I'm pleased to know that I'm not taking you away from anyone who would really appreciate you," Arabella told her, "for you're far too good for just general maid service."

"Will you need anything ironing for this afternoon or tonight, my lady?" Dora asked quietly as Arabella was about to leave the room.

She turned, looking thoughtfully at the maid as she tried to remember if her aunt had said anything about her plans. "I'm not sure yet about this afternoon, but I believe Lady Fitzwilliam mentioned that she was attending a musical evening. If that is the case, I'll take out the gown I wish to wear and leave it on the bed for you."

As she left the chamber and walked down the stairs,

Arabella realized that she had become completely unused to having a maid of her own and must remember to let Dora know her plans as far in advance as possible if she wished to be appropriately gowned.

Her papa and her aunt were in conversation at the foot of the stairs, and as Arabella approached them, her aunt saw her and smiled. "What a difference, my dear," she exclaimed. "That girl is quite a find. Turn around and let me see the back."

Arabella obediently turned around, grinning happily when her papa gave her a sly wink, then she dropped them a low curtsy. "Are you sorry that you did not keep her for yourself, Aunt Gertrude?" she asked teasingly.

"I'm past the age when it matters if a hair is out of place," Lady Fitzwilliam said, laughing. "It will be interesting to see if she handles your wardrobe as well as she does your hair."

"I'm sure she will, for she's already asked my plans for the afternoon and evening so that she can have the gowns ready," Arabella told her.

"She is good, then, for I'd forgotten to tell you that I'd like you to help me this morning with some invitations. I want to introduce you as soon as possible to some of my close friends, so I'm giving a small reception two nights from now," Lady Fitzwilliam said, feeling pleased with herself for conceiving the idea. "If you hurry with your breakfast, you can join me in the study and help me with the invitations and decide what we're going to serve. Then, this afternoon, we'll take them around when we go calling."

"I was just telling your aunt," Lord Darnley added, "that I have secured a box for us at the Drury Lane Theatre this evening. Edmund Kean is performing as Shylock, and I know you won't want to miss it, my dear."

"Oh, Papa, how did you know that was the one thing I wanted to see above anything else?" Arabella cried, giving her father a warm hug, and for a moment her thoughts strayed from Kean as she realized how much, these last six years, she had missed doing just that, for they had always been a demonstrative family.

"I've seen him a number of times," Lady Fitzwilliam said, "but I never tire of his performances. It's remarkable how such a small, quite ugly man can completely captivate everyone when he steps onto a stage."

"But what will I wear?" Arabella moaned. "My gowns are still being stitched at Madame Dubois."

"What nonsense! Go and eat your breakfast, young lady," her aunt told her firmly. "I'll send word to Madame that someone will be picking up the pale-green brocade this afternoon around four o'clock, and there's no question but that it will be waiting for us."

Arabella looked a little sheepish as she hurried into the breakfast room, for she recalled that only two days ago she had arrived here with just three black gowns to her name. Was she already becoming spoiled again?

Two hours later she did not feel at all spoiled, for she had been writing invitations for her aunt until her fingers ached. How could her dear relative have so many close friends?

"Just a half-dozen more, my dear, and then I think that will do very nicely," Lady Fitzwilliam said. "How many was it at last count?"

"Sixty-five," Arabella said disgustedly, "and you told me it was to be just a small affair."

"It is very small indeed by standards of the *ton*, my dear Arabella," Aunt Gertrude said a little severely, for, after all, she was going to all this trouble for her niece, not for herself. "And we'll probably have a little over fifty acceptances, even at this late date. If it were further along in the Season, we'd need to give everyone at least two weeks' notice and then expect only half of the people to be free."

"You're inviting them to a reception, Aunt Gertrude, but I'm not sure what that means. Do you intend to feed all your guests?" Arabella asked.

Lady Fitzwilliam looked amused. "Because you're already widowed I forget that you're such a green girl as far as society is concerned. Of course I will feed them all, as you so bluntly phrase it, but it will not be a formal dinner. In a few minutes, you and I will decide what kind of food to offer, but whatever it is, it will be served in the buffet-style, with the food set out on a large table for our guests to help themselves. They will take it to small tables, and a string quartet will play while they dine.''

"Where are you going to put all these people, Aunt Gertrude?'' Arabella asked. "Small tables will take up much more room than big ones.''

"In the ballroom, of course. Where else?'' Lady Fitzwilliam was becoming a little impatient, to say the least. What had got into the girl to ask such stupid questions?

"Do you mind if I ask what ballroom, Aunt Gertrude? I have not yet been shown the entire house, but did not think it large enough to contain a ballroom.''

"Oh, my dear, I'm so sorry. We've been so very busy ever since you arrived that I had completely forgotten you'd not been here before.'' Lady Fitzwilliam was on her feet in a moment. "Come along and we'll make up for that deficiency at once.''

It was a gracious house in an attractive square, and was much larger than it at first appeared from the outside. Arabella had been impressed by the wide staircase that divided halfway and went up again on each side, giving a grand display area for the portraits of the numerous Fitzwilliam ancestors. The largest and most extravagant of these was, of course, the one of the late marquess, and Arabella could not recall ever having seen a more unpleasant-looking gentleman.

"The artist was not quite accurate,'' Lady Fitzwilliam murmured as they passed. "He looked much worse than that in the flesh.''

Arabella glanced quickly at her aunt, who had preceded her up the staircase to the left, and wondered if she had really heard that remark or just imagined it.

"There are several guest rooms along here, and the largest one at the end is usually turned into a ladies' retiring room when the ballroom, just through the large double doors, is in use.'' Her aunt went forward and opened the door on the right, beckoning Arabella to follow. "It's an attractive room, as you see, and plenty large enough for a party five times the size.''

"Is that why they call such a party a crush?" Arabella could not help but ask, and her aunt just nodded and chuckled.

"Well, what do you think?" Aunt Gertrude's voice sounded gruff.

"I think your small reception will be the most elegant party of the Season, Aunt Gertrude, and I believe that's what you intend," Arabella answered. "Even though I have never been brought out, I have heard of Lady Sally Jersey, Mrs. Drummond Burrell, and Beau Brummell, to mention just a few of those you invited."

Lady Fitzwilliam, looking extremely pleased with herself, led the way back down the stairs and into the study. One of the things she had decided not to tell her niece was the fact that Lord Darnley had requested the addition of two names to the guest list, and she had written these herself.

She had no objections whatsoever to inviting Sir George Wetherby to her party, for she had met him on several occasions over the years and found him to be a most amiable gentleman. As for Lord Cavendish, if her brother said that the young man held no grudge against Arabella and that he felt his daughter would not at all mind seeing again the man to whom she had once been promised, who was she to argue against it?

Arabella, though married for five years, had never had a home of her own and had not, therefore, had experience in planning a party. To her it seemed a vast undertaking, but her aunt quickly assured her that it was nothing compared to the grand balls her friends would be giving when the Season was under way. Several hundred people would attend the most popular ones, she told her niece, for the hostesses took pride in having the biggest crush.

"And if a few of their guests die of suffocation before the end of the evening, what do they do?" Arabella asked in amusement. "Roll them up in a carpet and deposit them in their carriages?"

"You may laugh now, young lady," Lady Fitzwilliam said with a grim smile, "but if you're ever at one the Prince Regent attends, you might easily find yourself close to suffocation. He abhors drafts, you know, and so all windows and doors have to be kept closed while he is there.''

Arabella shuddered. ''I have no need to worry about that happening,'' she assured her aunt, ''for there is little chance I will meet up with him. I do not mean to go to balls while I am here, for I am not in the marriage market, and yet feel too young to be forced to sit with the chaperones and elderly ladies.''

To Arabella's surprise, her aunt agreed with her. ''The only thing to do at balls is to dance if you're young, or play cards if you're not, and I don't imagine you want to indulge in the serious card play that usually takes place. You've had enough of that to last a lifetime, I'll warrant,'' Aunt Gertrude said kindly. ''As a rule, I confine my social engagements to musical evenings, theater parties, dinners, and private card parties for small stakes.''

With the invitations written and some of them already put in the hands of Dawson, who would send reliable footmen out with them at once, the ladies were free to deliver the rest of them as they made their afternoon calls.

By the time they returned to Hanover Square, Arabella was convinced that the reception would be extremely well attended, for not one of Aunt Gertrude's many friends had declined. It had been a tiring afternoon, however, and they both retired to rest before dinner, for they did not want to miss any part of the performance tonight at Drury Lane.

As she stretched out on her bed to rest, Arabella saw that the pale-green brocade gown had arrived and was hanging on the outside of the armoire. She felt a twinge of excitement at the thought of wearing a beautiful evening gown of her own choice once again.

The gown still hung on the armoire when Arabella opened her eyes the next morning, but she knew that she had not dreamed the evening at the theater. She had been there, and worn the lovely gown, and marveled at Kean's performance as Shylock in *The Merchant of Venice*, seeking to have his pound of flesh.

The rest of the actors had served as little more than

background for Kean, and she had expected as much, for he was not known to appreciate competition for the audience's acclaim. The first part of the program had been a mishmash, and she and her aunt had readily agreed when her father suggested leaving immediately the curtain came down on the play.

While they waited in the vestibule for their carriage to be brought around, she had been introduced to several of her aunt's acquaintances who would be at the reception this evening, and now she had something else to look forward to, for it was the first time ever that a party had been given in her honor.

Soon that pale-green gown would be replaced by one in a lovely shade of almond that would be delivered today.

At the thought of all there was to be done before the party, Arabella sprang out of bed and tugged the bellpull for Dora. She could not be a slugabed today when her aunt would need all the help she could get.

She was right. From that moment on it seemed that she never stopped working at everything from running messages to helping move furniture, for no matter how much staff was employed, the right one never seemed to be about when needed. But at last Aunt Gertrude took a final look around the ballroom and other rooms that would be used tonight, and decided that everything was quite perfect. They could have tea and then lie down for a while before getting dressed for the reception.

"Madame Dubois is an artist," Lady Fitzwilliam declared when she came into Arabella's bedchamber to see how the new gown looked. "I was a little doubtful when she said that almond was the right color for you, but now I see how well it brings out the chestnut lights in your hair."

She was carrying a small box; she handed it to her niece and then said, a little gruffly, "I meant to give you these for a wedding present, but changed my mind when you married that scoundrel."

Arabella had to laugh at her aunt's words, but when she saw the contents of the box, the laughter died away. "Aunt

Gertrude, are these really for me?'' she sounded a little breathless.

''Of course they are, for you're better able to appreciate them now anyway. And they match the color of your eyes. Here, let me help you put them on, for if you drop one of the earrings, that cat of yours is sure to get it and hide it away.''

The box contained a matching sapphire necklace and earrings in an intricate gold setting, and they looked quite perfect against Arabella's creamy skin.

She hugged her aunt warmly, but was pushed away as the older lady mumbled, ''There's no time for that now, or the first guests will be in the hall before we are. And you know I'll have to rout out that brother of mine to stand with us.''

But Lady Fitzwilliam did not have to search for Lord Darnley. He was already waiting at the place agreed upon, and pride shone in his eyes when he looked at his little girl, now very much grown up.

The guests started to arrive almost at once, and for the next half-hour Arabella stood greeting her aunt's friends and trying to think of ways by which she would be able to remember each of their names.

She was smiling and talking to Lady Stafford when she saw Miles Cavendish coming toward her. She knew that her smile froze on her face, and hoped that the lady, who was a very dear friend of her aunt, did not notice.

He looked very handsome indeed, for his black hair, which was usually so unruly, was fashioned in a perfect *à la Titus,* and the ornate silver-handled cane he used added rather than detracted from his slightly rakish appearance. And there was no question that the slightly devilish glint in his gray eyes, beneath their thick black brows, made Arabella's pulse start to beat faster.

''How nice of you to come,'' she said automatically, for those were the words she had intoned at least thirty times this evening so far.

He took her hand and she felt the warmth and strength of his through her fine suede glove. ''How nice of you to invite me,'' he murmured in that deep, gravelly voice that had always sent shivers down her spine even when she was a little girl. "I'm happy to see you looking so very beautiful, my dear."

Suddenly she was tongue-tied, not knowing what to say next, but he seemed to understand for he said, "I don't believe you have met my uncle, Sir George Wetherby, who is an old friend of Lady Fitzwilliam."

He released her hand and she placed it in that of a tall and slim, scholarly-looking gentleman with a fine head of gray hair and a bright sparkle in his gray eyes.

"It is a pleasure to meet you at last, my lady," Sir George intoned, "for we have lived in the same neighborhood for the last year and never yet met."

Arabella found her voice at last. "Do you live with Miles at Warrington House, sir?" she inquired.

"I impose myself upon him, might be a better way of putting it," he said with a chuckle, "for I went there to keep an eye on things when he was off with Wellington's troops, and I liked it so much that I've never wanted to leave."

"Then you must know my father," Arabella said, turning to Lord Darnley, who was on her left.

"We're old friends, my dear," Lord Darnley said, and added a little sadly, "It's just you who have been away much too long."

They had to move away, for a line of people had formed behind them, but not before Miles had asked if he might take Arabella in to supper, and she had agreed before she had time to think about it.

After that the party became, to Arabella, a blur of happy, laughing people, many of whom had not seen one another since last Season and were catching up on the events of the winter.

She did not see Miles again until suppertime, when he seated her with her aunt while he and Sir George filled plates for them with the most delectable of foods, guaranteed to tempt the most jaded of appetites, which Arabella's certainly was not.

But the surprise of seeing Miles here seemed to have driven away her usual poise, and try as she may, she could not do more than make murmured responses to his efforts at polite conversation. She did not quite understand what was happening, for just his presence made her feel happy and excited, but something, perhaps her own guilty feelings at the way she had treated him, prevented her from relaxing and enjoying his company as she would have liked.

It was as if, one day, they would have to get together and talk seriously about what had happened in the past, before she could once more behave naturally with him.

7

"What a delightful lady," Sir George remarked as he and Miles Cavendish left Hanover Square in the small hours of the morning. "It's so rare to meet a widow who knows how to make a man comfortable yet does not fawn all over him. Do you not agree, Miles?"

Even in the dim light of the carriage Miles could see the look of satisfaction on his uncle's face, but he was puzzled, for though his own eyes had seldom left Arabella all evening, he could not, for the life of him, remember her having paid much attention to his uncle except at supper when he himself was with her.

"Completely, sir," he said warmly, "but I don't recall Arabella being in your company except when we first arrived and then, later, at supper."

"Arabella? She's a nice-enough chit, to be sure, but I meant her aunt, Lady Fitzwilliam," Sir George explained. "A charming woman if ever I saw one, and always was, as I recall. Can't think how she didn't turn sour married to an old curmudgeon like the late marquess. That young lady of yours does not know how lucky she is, for, with her aunt looking out for her, she's liable to become the toast of the town this Season."

Miles almost groaned, for it was the last thing he wished to happen. "She's already twenty-four, George," he protested, "and widowed under the worst of circumstances. However, she did look very lovely this evening. Don't you agree?"

Sir George edged deeper into his corner so that Miles could not see the grin on his face. "Completely. Dora told us she'd been well trained as a lady's maid, and it appears that she was telling the truth. Let's hope the girl's equally adept at finding out her mistress's engagements, or you may be spending your evenings at your club."

"Oh, I don't think that's very likely," Miles said with a little more confidence than he was feeling. "After all, in addition to Dora's investigative abilities, it appears I have an uncle who is more than a little interested in Lady Fitz-william. With your vast experience in the petticoat line, I'm sure you will be able to get a hint from her as to what functions she and her niece might be attending."

Sir George grunted. "Up to all the rigs, aren't you, young fellow? The poor chit don't stand a chance this time. How far did you get with her this evening, anyway?"

Miles had no intention of discussing his courtship of Arabella with his uncle, and was regretting that it had been necessary to tell him about it in the first place. However, there was little harm as yet, for as far as courtships went, this one had not even started.

"For a girl who hardly ever stopped talking at the age of eighteen, it would seem that Arabella has completely lost her tongue," he said ruefully. "But I have no doubt the condition will no longer prevail once she gets used to meeting me more often."

"She's probably still feeling embarrassed about the way she treated you before," Sir George suggested dryly. "As she sees more of you, that will disappear, I should think, and you may be sorry when it does."

"I doubt it," Miles said, "but taking everything into consideration, I'm quite pleased with the way things went. Now, if there's a note from Dora waiting when we get back, I will feel I've really made a start."

In actual fact, he already felt that he had made more than a start. He had wanted very much to put Arabella at ease this evening, but knew instinctively that the only way to do so would have been to sit down with her and talk quietly about everything that had happened six years ago. Neither the time nor the place was conducive to such a conversation. But his campaign was now under way. He had made a first foray and knew all too well that a subsequent tactical withdrawal before making another advance was usually the best stratagem.

On their return to the town house, George went directly to bed, but Miles checked to see if any messages had been received. He breathed a sigh of relief when he found a note from Dora waiting in the library. It was quite brief, simply informing him that tomorrow Arabella and her aunt would be attending a musical evening at the home of the Earl and Countess of Duncannon.

He reached for the pile of invitations that had accumulated already, shuffled through them, and quickly produced the right one. He would be there, despite his aversion to screeching sopranos, and he had little doubt that his uncle would accompany him after his remarks tonight about Lady Fitzwilliam.

As usual after the activities of a day, his leg was aching, and tonight it seemed worse than usual. He propped it up upon a footstool and began to massage the muscles of the thigh, which did not cure the problem but always seemed to give a modicum of relief.

That was something else he intended to do while in London. He had heard of a young doctor who had been remarkably effective in opening up old wounds and, if not curing, at least easing some of the pain so often experienced. In a few days he would inquire if this Dr. Radcliff was in town as yet, for word was that he only came here for a few months at a time. Then, once he had made some headway with Arabella, he would see if anything could be done at this stage with his old injury.

For now, however, a good night's rest would bring some

relief, so he wearily climbed the stairs and submitted to the ministrations of his valet, Vernon.

"A success, my dear, an unqualified success," Lady Fitzwilliam repeated as she joined her niece for morning chocolate, which was being served at a much later hour than usual because of last night's party.

"I thought it was a lovely party," Arabella told her aunt, who was sitting by the side of the bed wearing a lace sleeping cap and a flowing dressing gown. "But how do you know already that it was such a success?"

"The crowd, my dear," Lady Fitzwilliam said almost in awe, "for there were so many last-minute acceptances that we had to bring more tables into the ballroom to accommodate everyone. And then, the length of time they stayed. Do you realize that Sally Jersey was here almost to the end, and when she left, she told me how pleased she was with you and that vouchers to Almack's would soon be arriving."

Arabella tried to look suitably impressed while wishing that her aunt would go to her room and let her have a little more sleep. Then she noticed the letter that had been placed on the tray of hot chocolate.

Fortunately, her aunt had not seen it and was busily telling her how they must put in an appearance at Almack's next Wednesday evening, for they could not afford to offend the patronessess of that renowned establishment. Arabella had heard that before, so she was safe in just murmuring her agreement while she slipped the letter underneath the bedcovers.

"You know, for someone who used to accompany her husband while he played cards into the small hours of the morning, one late night seems to have taken a lot out of you, for you look quite tired this morning," Lady Fitzwilliam remarked, frowning a little. "Perhaps you'd better stay in bed and try to get a little more rest, my dear. I'll run along now and let you try to sleep. I'll have breakfast sent up to you in an hour or so, and you can get up at your leisure." She peered closely at her niece's pale face before turning around and hurrying from the chamber.

With a sigh of relief, Arabella drew the letter out from under the cover and used the back of a spoon to break the seal. She immediately realized she should not have done so, for now it was broken into small pieces and there was no way of knowing if the imprint had been recognizable.

She looked at the piece of paper, not touching it at first but taking another sip of her now-cold chocolate. Though she had been anxious for her aunt to go so that she could see the letter, she now felt a reluctance to unfold and read it, as though if she waited long enough it might just disappear before her eyes.

But it did no such thing, so she slowly opened up the sheet of paper. The printed words blurred before her eyes at first, then they came into focus: "SAPPHIRES MATCH THOSE COLD EYES. YOU WILL SEE ME SOON, AND THEN . . . "

Instinctively, Arabella's hands went to her throat where the necklace had been, and she shuddered. Who could be sending these letters? Had he been one of her aunt's guests? Or had he come in as one of the extra servants hired for the evening?

Now there was no more sleep in her, for her head was full of questions to which she had no answers.

There was a sound at the door, not the knock that would announce a servant or even her aunt, but a kind of rustle, and her heart began to pound. She watched as the knob slowly and silently turned, then the door started to edge open just a fraction at a time.

She slid out of bed and raced for the poker on the hearth, for she was not going to let him attack her without fighting back. Standing there, with the weapon firmly grasped in both hands and raised above her head, she waited for her attacker to come into view.

Then she heard a gasp, and from around the edge of the door a maid's cap appeared. It was no attacker but Dora's frightened face that came into view first, then the rest of her uniform.

"Oh, my lady, what on earth is the matter?" the girl asked fearfully, backing away from her mistress with a look of fear in her eyes, for she was sure Lady Arabella had gone mad.

Arabella looked at the poker, still held in her hands, then dropped it down onto the hearth. But the relief at finding it was only Dora was quickly followed by a fury she had not known herself capable of.

"Don't you ever come into this room without first knocking," Arabella shouted at the trembling girl, "or you'll be dismissed on the spot. Don't you realize that I could have killed you?"

"Yes, my lady," Dora whispered. "I'll not do it again. I was just trying not to waken you if you were sleeping, that's all."

The anger left as quickly as it had come, and Arabella sank into the chair near the bed, trembling, while tears started to roll down her cheeks.

Dora came quickly over and put her arms around her mistress, murmuring soothingly and wondering if she ought to fetch Lady Fitzwilliam. Then her eyes fell on the letter that was still lying face-upward on the bed. It was she who had placed it on the tray with the chocolate, and there had been a bit of a mystery belowstairs as to how it had arrived, for no one could recall it having been delivered to the house. The extra help hired for the evening was not supposed to answer the door, but one of them had probably done so, then left it in the hall.

As she read the message, she no longer wondered why her mistress had been so frightened. It looked like a threat to either steal the jewels or do something horrible to her.

"There, my lady," Dora said softly. "Don't take on so. I promise I'll never creep in and give you a scare like that again."

"I don't know which of us was the most frightened," Arabella said with a shaky laugh. "You must have thought I was a candidate for Bedlam, I'm sure."

She looked over to the bed and saw that she had left the letter there, but Dora's back was now to it and anyway, if she recalled correctly, the girl had told her that, like most of the servants, she could not read or write.

"I'm all right now, Dora," she said reassuringly. "What was it you came in for, anyway?"

"Just to see if you was awake and might like a bit of breakfast bringing up, my lady," the maid said. "It's almost time for luncheon, but an omelet and a little toast might just put you on till then."

"I really don't think I need anything, except perhaps a cup of coffee," Arabella said. "The food last night was so delicious that I just couldn't stop eating."

"Wasn't it just, my lady?" Dora agreed. "Her ladyship said we might have a few of the things that wouldn't keep overnight, and when we were finished putting everything away, we had a proper feast."

Arabella smiled as she rose and then quietly walked over to the bed, picking up the letter and then reaching for her writing case and tucking it in the back where the others were. Trying to sound casual, she asked, "Have you any idea when this note arrived?"

"It's a mystery, my lady," Dora was forced to admit. "Everyone swears they didn't take it in, but Mr. Dawson says it was sitting right there on the hall table after all the guests and hired help had gone and I was up here helping you to bed."

"Never mind, it's really not important," Arabella said, wishing it were only true. "I think the lavender gown with the violet trim would be suitable for the musical evening tonight. And I'll put on the blue carriage dress when I've had my coffee, for I'm sure my aunt will want to pay some calls this afternoon."

The maid hurried over to the armoire to get out the two garments, then left to take them down below and be sure they were in perfect order.

Once Dora was gone, Snowball came out to join Arabella. He sat on her lap, purring soothingly while she scratched his ears and stroked his soft fur. "Who could it have been?" she asked him as if he might have a solution to the problem. "Do you think it was one of the guests? I really don't think so, for Aunt Gertrude said she was inviting only her very best friends. Of course, someone could have come who was not invited. And then again he might have come as one of the extra hired help."

Snowball lifted his head and stared up at her as she suggested the latter.

"Is that what you think?" she asked him, then added, "I think so also, for it would have been very easy for him to hire on at an agency. How did he find out about the party, though? Aunt Gertrude only decided a couple of days ahead of time."

She kneaded his back, and his purring intensified. "But why is he doing this to me?" she asked. "Richard cheated and caused several men to lose an awful lot of money, but I didn't have any part of it. And I didn't get any of the money, either, for he always managed to lose it within a month or so."

Snowball let out a yelp and jumped down from her lap, turning around and glaring at her.

"Oh, dear," Arabella said, "I'm sorry. Was I being too rough with you?" She reached out to pick him up again, but he was not to be consoled and stalked away from her with his tail held high in the air, standing by the door and slipping out as Dora came in with the coffee. To his delight, he was now allowed the run of the house, but always came back to Arabella's chamber at night.

An hour later, when Arabella joined Lady Fitzwilliam in the dining room for luncheon, though she had not forgotten the unsigned note, she had at least put it to the back of her mind for now.

"How are you feeling, my dear? Rested, I hope, for we really must pay some calls this afternoon on some of the people who came last evening." Lady Fitzwilliam chuckled. "We'll be able to find out just what people are saying about my first party of the Season, and I will, of course, have to soothe the hurt feelings of any who feel they should have been invited and were not."

"I am completely rested, Aunt Gertrude," Arabella assured her, "and so I should be after spending almost all the morning abed. It must be more than a year since I slept so late, and I assure you I will not be making a habit of it."

"Of course you won't," her aunt said indulgently. "But after all, you worked all day to help me get everything done, and had no chance to take even a little rest before the first guests arrived. Did you solve the mystery of the letter for you that appeared out of nowhere? Dawson mentioned it to me this morning.''

''It was just a note from a distant relative of Richard's who would like to meet with me while I'm in town,'' Arabella said, making up the first thing she could think of. ''One of the servants hired for the evening must have taken it in, I suppose. Of course, I'll try to put it off as long as possible, for I have no wish to keep in touch with Richard's family.''

''I'm sure I don't blame you for feeling that way, my dear, for now you must do what's best for yourself. It's not as though you had children they might want to see. Take my advice and enjoy yourself while you can, Arabella,'' Lady Fitzwilliam said with a nod. ''And speaking of enjoying yourself, didn't Miles Cavendish pay you quite a lot of attention, considering everything that happened before?''

''He was just being polite, I believe, for he and Papa have known each other for a long time. I was about to ask you the same question about his uncle, for he seemed to spend quite some time in your company.'' Arabella grinned as she turned the tables on her aunt, but was surprised to see a rosy tint come to the older lady's cheeks.

In a back bedroom of a cheap lodging house just off Leicester Square, a man of about thirty years sat brooding and wondering why he had not burgled the house he was in the night before while he had the opportunity. After all, he could certainly use the money some of the baubles would have brought.

Then he shook his head in disgust. Was that what he, Viscount Alexander Galbraith, better known to his friends as Alex, had turned into—a common thief? And all because of his little brother, Timothy.

Tim had always been weak, he had to admit, and never seemed to quite get the hang of cards, though the Lord knew he played often enough. He had not at first believed Tim when he swore that he had not lost, but had been cheated out of everything he owned: the country estate their mother had left him, which would have kept them both in comfort for life, and the money that went with it, more than twenty thousand pounds.

Even after Tim killed himself, he, his big brother who should have known better, still wondered if the youngster had been telling the truth—that is, until he went up there and found out for himself.

Tim had told him there were two of them, the gambler and cheat, Sir Richard Barton and his beautiful wife, Lady Arabella Barton. She never played but wore enticing gowns and had looked at him, Tim swore, with promises in her big, sad eyes that completely took away a fellow's concentration on the game. She wore low-cut gowns with bits of lace and silk tucked in, Tim said, as though inviting you to pluck it out and see the rest.

His own trip up north, after he had buried his brother, had come a day or two too late. He'd stood there watching Barton using all the tricks of the trade to win the hands. But his opponent had not been a bantling this time, but a man in his prime, who had watched and waited until Barton fell into his trap and then he had told him loud and clear that he was a thief and a cheat.

Barton had jumped up at once and challenged the man, which had been what his opponent wanted, for he was obviously an excellent shot and had immediately named pistols—at dawn.

It had been unfortunate that in less than twelve hours after arriving from London, the man he had come to see and take his revenge upon for his brother's untimely death, was nothing but a corpse himself, quickly removed from the scene before a justice could appear and make an arrest.

But Barton's wife was still alive! Lady Arabella Barton was now a widow, and judging by her demeanor as she made the necessary arrangements to convey her husband's body to the family graveyard many miles to the south, she might have done this kind of thing every day of the week. Widow's weeds, yes, but a cold bitch who shed not a single tear nor showed a hint of emotion. It would have been interesting to see her face when she received his first letter. Did it show fear? Or did it show contempt? She must at least have wondered which of their many victims was bothering her now!

Alex had followed the coffin rather than the woman, which had been his first mistake, for once she reached her destination, Barton's sister and her husband never let her out of their sight. But at least he'd sent another threat, in an attempt to make her squirm a little while he waited to take his revenge. He got a bit of satisfaction then, though, for he helped dig the bastard's grave and even got paid for it!

But he almost lost her when she came to London, for it was only by chance that he heard she had left the north and taken the stage. A grim smile twisted his face when he recalled the scene at the inn yard. What poetic justice it would have been had Mother Gordon succeeded! And she would have if that big fellow hadn't been there with his hackney.

I have no money, she'd said, opening wide her blue eyes, and the cabby had fallen for her act at once.

He'd had to creep dangerously close to hear where she was going, but it had been worth it, for she'd given away both the name and the address.

What a surprise she must have got when his first letter arrived. It was a pity he couldn't have seen her face, but he'd got such a goodly amount of satisfaction when he heard how puzzled the staff and that starchy butler were about where it had come from. The little maid who was his contact inside the house was enjoying it as much as he was himself, and he knew it would drive them crazy if more letters just appeared the same way, out of nowhere.

And there would be more, three or four at least before he took the revenge he sought.

8

"Of what exactly does a musical evening consist?" Arabella asked as she and her aunt settled back against the squabs of the carriage and set out for the Earl and Countess of Duncannon's house in Berkeley Square. Lord Darnley had declined to escort them this time, giving a snort of disgust when the entertainment was made known to him.

"It will probably start with a pianist or violinist rendering some classical pieces," her aunt told her, "and then, if we're lucky, a buffet supper will be served."

"Is that all? Then why did Papa refuse to join us?" Arabella asked, for it sounded perfectly pleasant to her.

A low chuckle came from her aunt's corner of the carriage. "He has probably been to such entertainments when the daughters of the house have rather ineptly performed, or when the professional singers, particularly the sopranos, were not the easiest upon the ears." She paused, choosing her words carefully. "And then there are evenings when the hostess provides just one entertainer, probably a pianist, and seeks talented guests to show off their accomplishments."

"Oh," Arabella said, and there was silence for a moment before she went on. "Perhaps in the future I should ask such a question before the invitation is accepted."

"And perhaps you shouldn't, young lady," her aunt said abruptly. "There are times when one has to accept an invitation not because the evening will be enjoyable but because the hostess is a good friend or has performed some service for you."

There was a sharpness in her aunt's voice that Arabella had seldom heard, and she was immediately ashamed of herself for her thoughtless remark.

"I feel I have been given a well-deserved set-down, Aunt Gertrude." Her voice held a note of sincere remorse. "Were it not for you and your good friends I would be staying home every evening." She paused, then begged earnestly, "Would you at least assure me, dear Aunt, that I will not be expected to get up and perform tonight, for I know that were I to do so, despite their obligations, half the people there would immediately find some excuse to leave."

Lady Fitzwilliam reached across and patted her niece's hand, then told her a little gruffly, "There are occasions, my dear—fortunately not very many of them—when I deeply regret not having a daughter of my own. At the time, however, I did not wish to produce a child from the old marquess's stock. You have done much to make up for my loss, but I only wish I could have brought you out six years ago, as we planned."

"So do I," Arabella said with feeling, "and I paid very dearly for that mistake, so don't let's talk about it now. Do the Duncannons have children who will be performing tonight?"

"They have a daughter who I believe is quite talented— and also one who is not, but I'll not tell you which one is which. You'll have to decide that for yourself," Lady Fitzwilliam said with a laugh. "And now we are there, and I believe that is Sir George Wetherby just going up the steps with Lord Cavendish. I am surprised to see them, for I would not have thought either one of them musically inclined."

As they stepped out of the carriage, the two gentlemen turned around, then waited to escort the ladies inside.

"What a coincidence," Sir George said heartily, "and

what perfect timing! Unless someone is already saving seats for you ladies, I would be delighted if we might sit together.''

"It would be our pleasure, Sir George," Lady Fitzwilliam said quickly before her niece could make any excuse. "I didn't know that you were interested in music.''

He leaned toward her. "I'll make a confession. I'm not at all fond of the stuff," he told her with a grin. He glanced across to be sure that his nephew could not hear, then added, "It was Miles who wanted to come, for he's a great music lover, I'll have you know, and I'd not let him come alone and be at the mercy of all those marriage-minded mamas."

As they moved along to the receiving line, which consisted of the Earl and Countess of Duncannon and their two daughters, Arabella could not help but wonder which of the girls was the talented one, for they both looked too timid to enjoy performing in public.

Once the formalities were over, Sir George found four seats together toward the back of the room, a small couch for the ladies, with a chair on either side for the men. They took their places at once, for a violinist was already tuning up and the performance was about to begin.

"I don't recall that you were fond of music, Arabella," Miles remarked quietly, "and I'd almost swear that Richard detested any he could not dance to."

"You're quite right," she agreed. "He was not at all musically inclined. And I must admit that I'm not much better than he was, for Papa did not insist I learn to play an instrument when I made my objections known. But, you see, because I did not have a formal come-out . . ." She stopped speaking suddenly and went quite pink as she recalled the reason why this had not occurred.

Miles quickly realized the cause of her discomfort and tried to put her at ease. "Don't let the past bother you, my dear," he murmured in her ear. "Try to think of us as just good friends who have met again after much too long a time."

As he leaned toward her, she felt his warm breath on her cheek and found herself enjoying his nearness, though his words did not quite take away her embarrassment. The ex-

citement she had felt in his presence the last time was still
there, but now she determined that she was not going to be
so tongue-tied again.

"I was trying to explain why I do not know many ladies
of my own age in London. Because of this, I leave it
completely to my aunt to decide which invitations we should
accept. She and Papa have been wonderful to me since I
arrived here," she told him, "and I'm only sorry now that
I did not come here sooner."

"The estrangement from your father must have been most
distressing to you, for I clearly recall how fond of him you
always were," Miles said gently, then added, "and he of
you."

"Yes, and I never stopped feeling that way. He was both
mama and papa to me, you know, for I have no recollection
of my mother at all," she admitted. "Now it's just as though
my life is beginning again."

"The years of your marriage were good ones, though,
weren't they?" he suggested. "Surely the two of you were
in love, or you'd not have run away?"

Arabella looked at him and shook her head. "I'd never
seen Richard alone until he appeared that night at the inn.
He was jealous of you," she said simply, "and he wanted
me because I was yours. He also thought he would get my
dowry, of course, but Papa was wise enough not to give it
to him."

Although they were speaking quietly so that no one could
hear what they were saying, the people in front looked around
at the murmur of voices, and when Lady Fitzwilliam gave
Arabella a warning nudge, further conversation was
impossible.

The violinist was quite talented, but Miles was unaware
of it as he thought about those wasted years. He had always
thought they had been secretly seeing each other. Now he
felt a silent rage at the villainy of his former friend, for
Richard's note to Lord Darnley had said they had been lovers
for some time and could no longer stay apart. He wondered
if Arabella had ever seen that note, which had changed his
entire life.

The audience was applauding and he joined in automatically, assuming that the performance was finished. Encouraged, the violinist gave an encore, but this was soon over and the first part of the program, at least, came to an end.

When the rest of the people rose to go into the refreshment room, Miles suddenly found that he had a problem. He had known that a straight wooden chair was the worst thing for him to sit upon, and now his bad leg had stiffened. He would have to massage it for some time before he could persuade it to even partially support his weight. Motioning for George, who had seen this happen before, to take the ladies inside, he said, "I'll come in as soon as I can."

"Does the leg pain him very much, Sir George?" Arabella asked as they made their way into the refreshment room.

"I'm afraid he has almost constant pain from it," he told her sadly, "but it is, of course, worse after he sits for any length of time on a hard surface."

"Then he must have known what would happen before he even sat down," she protested. "Why did he not say something? We could have looked for other seats."

"Because he is first and foremost a gentleman, Arabella, and would not have thought of putting you ladies to any inconvenience," he said firmly. "You were more than well acquainted with him at one time, and should know that."

Arabella flushed painfully. "Can't anything be done to make it more comfortable?" she asked, persevering with her questioning despite her embarrassment.

Sir George shrugged. "Who can tell? Once we're a bit more settled here, he's going to see a doctor he's heard of who has been able to help such cases. It may be too late, of course, but then again it may not. But don't tell him I told you this, young lady, for he would not like me discussing it with you."

Arabella opened her mouth to ask something else, but her aunt gave her a little nudge.

"How did you enjoy the violinist, my dear?" Lady Fitzwilliam asked her a little pointedly. "Quite a talented young man, I thought."

"Excellent," Arabella said, then asked with a wicked smile, "Are we to hear the daughters of the house after supper?"

"At least one of them, I'm afraid," Lady Fitzwilliam admitted, smiling quite mischievously. "And probably quite a few other talented young people. You did say you would sing, as I recall, didn't you?"

Arabella looked horrified. "Don't you dare tell them such a lie, or you'll most surely regret it," she threatened, but her aunt just laughed.

As soon as the music room was empty except for servants, Miles had begun to steadily massage his leg, and it was not too long before he was able to limp toward the supper room. Now he stood in the doorway looking to see where his companions might be, and was heartened when he saw Arabella waving a kerchief to attract his attention.

"Good girl," he said with a smile. "I might have been the rest of the evening trying to find you in this crush."

Arabella was surprised at the pleasure she felt by just those first two words. "We also saved some food for you," she told him, smiling and placing a plate of various savories and pastries in front of him.

But she looked very serious as she watched him take a bite, and finally asked, "Won't that happen again if you sit down on that hard chair?"

"I'm afraid so," he said ruefully. "Perhaps I'd best stand at the side of the room, or I may find myself staying at the Duncannons' all night."

"Wouldn't it be better if you sat on the upholstered sofa instead," she suggested practically. "I wouldn't at all mind sitting on the chair, and I would hate to see you stand for the rest of the evening."

"An excellent idea, my girl," Aunt Gertrude put in, completely staring Miles out of countenance. "You seem to prefer a hard chair much of the time, if I recall."

"I see I'm outflanked and must give in gracefully," Miles said, though his voice was a little gruff, for he did not at all care for the fuss that was being made.

They had not reckoned with their most considerate hosts,

however, for when they returned to their seats they found that a second sofa had been substituted for the two chairs and Miles did not have to accept Arabella's offer, after all.

The second half of the entertainment had not yet started, giving Miles the opportunity he had been waiting for to pose a question to Arabella.

"You used to love to ride, as I recall, yet I never saw you mounted during the year you just spent in the north. Do you no longer like riding?"

"I haven't ridden since . . ." She bit her lip hesitantly. "Since before I left home, Miles. You see, we were never settled anywhere long enough to do anything like that. Richard had his curricle, and that's how we usually went from place to place. I probably don't know how to anymore."

He gave a short laugh. "Once you learn to ride, it's something you never forget. Could I, perhaps, persuade you to come riding in the park with me one morning? I'd bring a mount and a groom for you, so you'd have no excuse," he warned.

"I've the best excuse in the world, I'm afraid, for I have no riding habit, Miles," she said, extremely sorry to have to turn down his invitation, for she would have dearly loved to ride again.

"That's no excuse at all." Lady Fitzwilliam had overheard the conversation. "I have one that no longer fits me, but will be just right for you, so if you want to see for yourself if you can still ride, it's yours," she told her, thinking to herself that her niece must have had a most peculiar married life. No wonder she didn't speak of it often.

Miles grinned boyishly at Arabella and raised an eyebrow. "Will tomorrow morning at eight o'clock suit you?" he asked.

"I think we'd better make it the following morning, just in case my aunt's habit is a little long, for she is taller than I am," Arabella said, smiling happily at the thought of being on horseback again. "I hope Dora is handy with a needle and thread."

Miles had difficulty stopping himself from telling her that

of course she was, for when the girl had first started working for him, she had been put to helping the housekeeper mend linens. Dora would have that riding habit shortened in no time at all, he knew.

But Arabella did not have to wait until they went riding to see him again, for when she and Lady Fitzwilliam attended a small reception the next night, given by another of her aunt's good friends, Miles Cavendish and Sir George Wetherby were there before them.

She told herself she was pleased on her aunt's account, for that lady seemed to enjoy the company of Sir George very much, but in truth she was finding Miles to be much more intelligent, more amusing, and more courteous than the other men she met. In fact, though there were many other gentlemen who had now started to pay her attention, none of them could compare in the slightest with Miles.

Promptly at eight o'clock the next morning, he was waiting with his groom and a quite lively little chestnut filly that Arabella fell in love with at once. She did not know, of course, that Miles had bought the horse at Tattersall's a few days ago, especially for her use.

The park was quiet at that hour, and they were able to gallop without being observed, and Arabella found that Miles had been right, as usual, for she might be a little sore afterward, but she rode as naturally as though she had never stopped.

They slowed to a trot, taking a quiet path close to some trees, leaving the groom a considerable distance behind, and Miles turned to get a good look at Arabella's face, which seemed alight with pure joy.

"There's one thing I have to ask you, Arabella, for it's been puzzling me for the past two days. If you had not had a previous relationship with that bounder before you left for London, why did you run away with him?" He hated to see the pleasure leave her face at his question, but he had to know.

She made no attempt to avoid answering, but her voice held a distinct note of bitterness as she replied, "Because I had been young and silly enough to believe I could have a light flirtation with him in a private parlor at an inn where he had just happened to also be staying.'' She paused and looked at Miles with sadly disillusioned eyes. "He planned it all, of course. Found out where I would be stopping, bribed my abigail to pretend to be sick, and the innkeeper to tell me there was no other private parlor he could use."

"And then what did he do?" Miles was trying hard to control his fury.

"He kept refilling my wineglass and dared me to have brandy. You may possibly remember how foolish I was in those days about accepting dares," she said with a sad shake of her head. "I'm sure he didn't drag me out of the inn and into his curricle, but I was too intoxicated to know what I was doing until the next morning, when we were already well on the way to the Scottish border. I felt quite sick, of course, even before he said I had allowed him to compromise me and there was nothing to be done but get married." She gave a little shrug, for it was really no longer important to her.

"And had he . . . ?" Miles began, but Arabella anticipated his question and gave a slight shake of her head.

"No, he hadn't. I found to my surprise that night that I was still a virgin, but he had sent word to my papa and it was, without a doubt, too late by then to save my reputation." She reined in the filly and looked at the man she had injured so badly, who was gazing at her with a strange expression on his face.

"It wasn't," he said softly. "I would have taken you back and helped put the gossip to rest by marrying quietly."

They looked at each other for a few moments, both knowing the truth of what he said.

"It might not have worked even then, Miles." She disliked telling him, but it was better he know the truth. "I was silly and young for my age, and I needed to grow up and face life. Richard made me do that, none too gently, and I hated him for it. What if I had hated you?"

He reached over and gave Arabella's hand a squeeze. "You wouldn't have," he said, then he smiled. "I didn't mean to bring you out here and make you recall a lot of things you'd sooner forget. Let's leave it for now and have another gallop while we still have the place to ourselves.''

The wind in her hair blew away the past as Arabella raced alongside Miles for as long as the little filly could keep up, then she dropped back and marveled at the joy she could still get from something she had once taken completely for granted. Perhaps, at the end of the Season, Miles would sell this little beauty to her father.

As soon as Miles realized she had dropped back, he reined in his own horse until he was alongside her once more, then he suggested that she might like to take a stroll through the pretty wooded area to their right.

She readily agreed, so he dismounted and helped her down, and they walked the horse slowly toward the copse, where he tied both mounts to trees a little distance apart.

Taking her hand in his, Miles led her along a narrow path with primroses blooming on either side until they were out of sight of any prying eyes, then he turned her toward him, placing a hand on each of her shoulders and drawing her close.

Arabella could feel his breath as it mingled with hers in the cool early-morning air.

"I've waited a long time to do this, my dear," he said softly as he drew her closer. His soft lips brushed lightly over hers, tasting their coolness, then he drew back, unsure of her response.

She did not try to pull away, nor did she move closer, for she was completely stunned at her reaction to such a friendly, gentle kiss, for it had seemed as though a fire had started deep down inside of her.

His fingers lightly stroked her cheek and she felt herself shudder with pleasure, then his lips were back, hungry this time, demanding a response. Suddenly, though she'd never known of its existence, a deep passion rose within her and she felt a desire racing through her that she'd never thought possible.

Momentarily frightened at its power, she pulled away and he released her lips immediately, keeping his hands behind her shoulders in case her balance was not quite steady. She could not believe that she was actually trembling because of a single kiss. Comforted by his strength, she rested her cheek against his chest, still breathing heavily and still afraid—but of herself, not him.

When her heartbeat returned to normal, she reluctantly drew away, smoothing her ruffled hair with her hands and straightening her shako, but not daring yet to look up into his face.

Miles was almost as shocked as she was, for though he had silently demanded a response, when it came, he had not been prepared for the intensity of it. He studied her downcast eyes for a moment longer, then took her hand in his and led her back to where the horses waited. After giving her a leg up, he mounted himself, but before moving he put a hand on her rein and gave her a long look to be sure she really was all right.

In silence they turned and made their way slowly back to the entrance.

"I have my phaeton in town," he said after a while, "and was wondering if, one of these fine afternoons, you and your aunt might like to take a drive in the park or wherever else you might fancy."

Arabella smiled faintly, then made a tremendous effort to lighten the mood. "Isn't that the thing to do on an afternoon—drive through the park and nod or stop to visit with all your friends and acquaintances?" she asked with a forced brightness.

He managed a grin. "It is one of the favorite pastimes of the *ton*," he agreed.

"I'll have to ask Aunt Gertrude, of course, but I don't think there will be much doubt about her accepting your invitation, for I know she does not own an open carriage."

"Will you be at the Winterfords' card party tonight?" he asked. "If you are going, then I'll ask her myself and we can decide upon a suitable afternoon."

"Why, yes, that is where we're going tonight," Arabella said, still too shocked by her own hidden feelings to be surprised that they were going to the same friends' home once more.

They caught up to the groom before they reached the entrance to the park, and rode the rest of the way in a slightly uncomfortable silence, for Miles, though delighted for himself at her warmth and passion, recognized her fear and knew that she would have to come to terms with it herself. She needed time to get used to it, and he was quite prepared to give her that, provided the outcome was all right.

Miles did not come in, but helped her dismount, then waited until she was inside the house before leaving.

Arabella hurried up the stairs and into her room. She knew that her aunt would have heard her come in and expect her down soon for breakfast, but first she needed a moment to herself.

For someone whose husband had called her a cold bitch the first time he had taken her to bed, and had continued to do so at intervals throughout the years of their marriage, she had just revealed a remarkable hidden fire.

The very idea took a lot of getting used to, and she was still not sure whether she liked it or not, but it was there and it would be interesting to find out if it would stay.

9

The morning had been an exhausting one, and Miles now half-regretted his promise to take Arabella and Lady Fitzwilliam for another drive in the park this afternoon. He would, he knew, be much more comfortable if he could just stretch out on his own bed for a few hours.

His meeting with Dr. Radcliff had been somewhat unexpected, for he had paid a visit to the Royal College of Physicians in order to ascertain the whereabouts of the young doctor and found that he was, by chance, in the building at the time.

Showing Miles into a private room, Dr. Radcliff had asked him to take a seat and had then perched on a corner of the examining table while he found out as much as he could about the extent and treatment of the original wound.

"What bad luck that you had to catch it at Toulouse," he had said sympathetically. "It's a wonder we didn't meet then, for I was there, but I'm sure I would have remembered had I treated you. Officers got priority in my book, but only so that they could get back in the field and lead their men. Let's get you on the table and take a look."

For the next half-hour he had poked and pushed and

probed, flexed the knee and straightened it until beads of perspiration were standing out on Miles' forehead.

But it had been worth it, for in the end Dr. Radcliff said apologetically, "I'm sorry to have to put you through that, but it was necessary. I believe I can help you. It will, however, involve more surgery and you'll have to be prepared to work very closely with me afterwards to be sure everything heals right this time. Are you willing to give it a try?"

"That's why I looked you up," Miles replied shortly. "How long will you be in town, for I assume that once it's done, I'll be out of commission for some time? You see, Doctor, I'd like to make a little more progress with a special project I'm engaged in, before being laid up."

The doctor grinned. "I think we'd deal better if you called me Tom and I used your first name. After all, though we never met, we were in the same war together."

This was much preferable from Miles' point of view. He had liked the young doctor on sight, and he readily agreed.

"Now, Miles, your special project at the beginning of a London Season sounds to me as though it concerns a lady. And you know as well as I do that it could take the whole Season to come to a satisfactory conclusion," Tom Radcliff said, knowing by the look on the other man's face that he had guessed correctly. "I will have about six more weeks here before I must return north, and I'll need to work closely with you for at least a month after the surgery."

"That gives me two more weeks, then, Tom. You're very astute, but I'll tell you frankly that I have no intention of staying here the whole Season. I can't, for I've too much to do up north. I'd hoped to conclude a successful campaign of mine within the month, and then have the surgery." Miles pursed his lips as he considered the problem. "How soon would I be on my feet again?"

Tom Radcliff gave him a measured look, for he realized he was dealing with a very determined man who would probably try to go even faster than he should.

"You'd be on your feet in a week," he told him, "but putting practically no weight upon the leg at first. I'd give you exercises to perform daily with the help of your man, but you'd have to go at the pace I set or you'd undo all my work. I'll tell you frankly, Miles, I won't even take you as a patient unless I have your word that you'll obey my instructions to the letter.''

"I can't blame you for that, Tom. I'd do exactly the same if I was in your shoes. However, I'm not," Miles said a little grimly. He knew he would feel completely frustrated if he could not continue to see Arabella, but he did not want her near him while he was incapacitated and most certainly short-tempered because of it. That would ruin everything. "At the end of the month would I be able to put reasonable weight on the leg?" he asked thoughtfully.

Tom nodded. "Yes, but with emphasis on the reasonable. You'd not be able to run or jump around at that stage, but eventually you should be able to indulge in such performances if they appeal to you," he said with a grin. "Why don't you think about it and let me know in a day or two what you decide?"

They had shaken hands and Miles had left the building deep in thought. There was no question but that he wanted Tom Radcliff to operate. It was just a matter of when. Why had he waited until so long to find out about him? he asked himself. He could have made a special trip and the whole thing would be over with by now.

But it was almost time to pick up the two ladies in Hanover Square, so he rose painfully to his feet and started for the door, almost bumping into his uncle, who was just returning from a visit to his tailor.

"I say, old fellow, sit down for a moment, won't you?" Sir George said in alarm as he saw the pain on his nephew's face. "What happened?"

Miles tried to shake off his uncle's hand on his arm. "I'll explain later. Right now I'm promised to Arabella and Lady Fitzwilliam," he said, glowering, "taking them for a ride in the park."

"You're not fit to take them anywhere," Sir George said sharply. "Why don't you let me take them instead, and you can go and lie down—after you've told me what's wrong."

It was a solution Miles had not thought of, and he looked at his uncle with relief. "Would you mind, George? And give Arabella my profound apologies. You see, I saw the doctor I told you about this morning, and his examination was extremely thorough," he said with a barely suppressed groan. "But you'd best leave now if you're not going to be late. The phaeton will be out front in just a moment."

"The ladies are not a pair of young ninnyhammers who throw tantrums if a fellow's a few minutes late," Sir George snapped. "I'm going to get Vernon and give him a hand with you up the stairs."

He went into the hall and gave an order, and within a few minutes Miles' man appeared, looking horrified when he saw his master's face.

"It's all right, don't make such a fuss, the pair of you," Miles admonished. "The fellow had to test it thoroughly to see just how much movement I have in it now. He's a good man and he's going to fix it."

Nothing further was said until the two of them had helped get Miles up the stairs and stretched out on his bed. Then Miles smiled weakly and said, "Make something up to satisfy them, George, that's a good fellow."

Sir George smiled grimly and nodded at the servant. "Take good care of him, Vernon. A dose of laudanum might not be amiss."

Fifteen minutes later, he drew the phaeton up outside the home of Lady Fitzwilliam and gave the reins to the groom. "Walk them," he said, "for we'll be a few minutes yet, I believe."

He was shown into the drawing room, where both ladies were elegantly gowned for their ride in the park, Arabella in a carriage dress of the softest shade of green, and her aunt in one of silver gray trimmed with wine velvet. Their hats were frothy concoctions, matching their gowns and designed to catch the eye of everyone they met. Lady Fitzwilliam smiled and raised her eyebrows.

"Miles sends his apologies, my ladies, and he expects me to make up an excuse, but I believe that you're both sensible enough for me to tell you the truth without having to wrap it up in fine linen," he said.

He quickly explained about Miles' leg injury and his visit to a doctor this morning.

"But surely he won't let a man operate on him who is so rough in his examination?" Lady Fitzwilliam suggested.

Sir George shook his head. "He wasn't rough, according to what Miles told me. He had to find out just how much he could and could not do with it, and I can tell you myself that the boy can't hardly move it an inch without being in pain," he avowed. "If I hadn't arrived in the nick of time, he'd have come here and tried to take the two of you out— just because he'd promised."

"I can understand that, for he's a perfect gentleman," Lady Fitzwilliam said. Then she added for her niece's benefit, "Some young lady is going to be very fortunate indeed when Miles finally decides to take a wife."

Arabella said nothing, for she suddenly felt an overwhelming desire to go to Miles and take care of him. She knew she couldn't, for society would indeed frown on such a thing and quickly bring up her past misdeeds. She did not quite understand her feelings now, for when she had been married to Richard she had not once had even the slightest desire to look after him. But, then, she had not loved Richard, she thought. Did it follow that she loved Miles? she wondered. She realized she always had, in a sisterly sort of way, but since that startling kiss in the park she had not felt at all sisterly toward him.

Miles was now behaving as though nothing unusual had happened that morning, but she felt as though she was on a seesaw, happy one moment and unhappy the next. But whatever her feelings, gay or sad, nothing could come of them while the threats continued, for she would not allow Miles to be hurt again.

The park was alive with members of the *ton* taking the air. It was a delightful spring afternoon, and a great many people had descended upon London these past few weeks. Arabella no longer felt like a stranger from the north, for she had now met quite a lot of people, and it was most pleasant to be able to acknowledge friends of her own and not just those of her aunt.

Sir George suddenly uttered an exclamation, then steered the phaeton in the direction of one driven by a beautiful young woman who looked as happy to see him as he was to see her. A small boy and a nanny sat beside her.

"George, how nice to see you in town again," the black-haired beauty cried. "Miles told me the other day that you were here."

"Ladies, permit me to introduce my niece, Lady Cloverdale, and her young son, Charles. Audrey, this is Lady Fitzwilliam and her niece, Lady Arabella Barton." Busy with the introductions, Sir George did not notice the look that his niece shot at Arabella.

"I believe we have met before," Lady Cloverdale said coldly to Arabella. "Aren't you the Lady Arabella Darnley who was to have married my cousin and then ran off with someone else?"

Now Arabella knew who this lovely young matron was. She was the little cousin who sometimes came to visit Warrington House in the summer and who had worshiped Miles and hung on to his every word. This was bound to happen one day, she told herself, then lifted icy blue eyes to return the younger woman's glance.

"Yes, I am," she said quietly. "And I remember you now, for you must be Audrey, who came to visit and loved Miles to the exclusion of everyone else. How much more rewarding it must be to have a delightful young son on whom to lavish your affection."

"Thank you," Lady Cloverdale said gruffly, placing an arm around the boy as though to protect him and wondering why she was thanking the woman she had never liked. "Does Miles know she is in town, George?"

"You are being extremely rude, Audrey," Sir George said sternly. "Miles and Arabella are still good friends, and he would not appreciate your remarks."

Not even attempting to hide her resentment at the reproach, the young matron glared at them all, then with a toss of her head she deftly steered her carriage to the right and started out at trot, slowing her pace slightly only when she remembered where she was.

"I must apologize for my niece's bad manners, ladies," Sir George said, noticing the nervous way in which Arabella's fingers were twisting the handle of her reticule. "Had I realized she had not yet learned how to behave, I would never have taken you over to meet her. I can assure you that Miles will give her a severe scold when next they meet."

That was the last thing Arabella wanted, and she said quickly, "Please don't tell him, Sir George. I'm sure she will have already forgotten she ever saw me."

Lady Fitzwilliam did not feel quite so lenient, however. "I'm afraid that she may start some trouble for you, my dear, so it would be better if Miles did speak to her. There was enough gossip about the duel last year, without the *ton* being informed of a past scandal."

"Your aunt is quite right, my lady," Sir George said to Arabella. "As the betrothal was not official, only very close family knew about it. To have it talked about now would be most embarrassing to both you and Miles. He will know how to deal with her, I am sure."

"If you think it best, then," Arabella said quietly. "But is Miles in any fit state to handle it at the moment?"

Sir George patted her hand in a fatherly fashion. "Now, don't you go treating Miles like an invalid, my dear, or he'll realize I told you all about it and be furious with me. I would be willing to wager that he'll be up and about before I get back, and will see you at the Casterfields' reception this evening." He realized he had said a little too much and quickly corrected himself. "That is, of course, if you and Lady Fitzwilliam are attending, as we are."

"We wouldn't miss it, Sir George," Lady Fitzwilliam told him. "Lady Casterfield's brother, for whom the reception is being given, is a well-known poet in his own circle, and in addition it is rumored that his friend, Lord Byron, might also attend."

Sir George now recalled very clearly his own and Miles'

reaction when the note from Dora arrived, telling them of the ladies' plan to attend this particular occasion. Miles had groaned audibly and told him that there was no need for both of them to go through such an ordeal. But they had decided that the ladies deserved their support and promptly sent Lady Casterfield their acceptance.

Arabella was now looking at him in a most peculiar way, for she found it difficult to believe that he and Miles were at all interested in poetry.

Noticing her expression, Sir George said hastily, "It's not much to Miles' taste, of course, but I used to pen a little verse myself when I was not much more than a stripling. He was just going to please me, so I'm sure he'll be delighted to know that you will both be there." He withdrew a handkerchief from a pocket and hastily mopped his brow.

"How very interesting. Perhaps you could . . ." Lady Fitzwilliam began, smiling a little naughtily, but Sir George was saved from whatever suggestion that lady was about to make by a hail from one of her bosom bows.

Much to his relief, the rest of the drive was taken up by greeting first one and then another of their acquaintances, and by the time they returned to Hanover Square the ladies had forgotten all about his professed forays into the realm of verse.

As Sir George had expected, by late afternoon Miles was completely recovered from the morning's exertions and did, in fact, after hearing of the incident in the park, pay an immediate call on his cousin Audrey and gave her a scold so severe that she canceled her plans for the evening and retired in tears to her bedchamber.

The entertainment provided by the Casterfields was not at all to his taste, and he had difficulty at times in keeping a pained expression from his face, but when he slipped up and allowed a grimace to appear, the ladies generously attributed it to pain from his leg injury.

"Lady Casterfield just told me how excited she is that Lord Byron is really coming here this evening," Lady Fitzwilliam announced as Miles and Sir George joined her and Arabella at a small supper table. "She feels most fortunate, of course, that he thinks enough of her brother to put in an appearance here when he will so soon be leaving the country."

"I wonder if he is really as handsome as people say," Arabella remarked, "for I have heard that his crippled foot does not detract from but enhances his appeal."

Sir George glanced at Miles and noted his expression of distaste, then turned to follow his nephew's gaze. "Judge for yourself, my dear," he told the ladies, "for there's the young man who has been the cause of much scandal over the years, standing near the door and talking now to his hostess."

The heads of both ladies turned in that direction where a dark-haired, broody-looking man stood listening intently to Lady Casterfield. A few minutes later he was joined by her brother, who had provided the evening's entertainment thus far, and the two men moved slowly in the direction of the supper table. Lord Byron's limp was clearly evident, but seemed to enhance rather than detract from his appearance.

"Do you suppose that he really is insane, as Annabella Millbanke claims?" Lady Fitzwilliam asked. "He looks much like a great many other young men of his generation to me, except, of course, for his leg."

"It has become fashionable for some young men to emulate him, my dear," Sir George explained. "His good friend, Lady Melbourne, would hardly have promoted his marriage to her niece had she considered his sanity in doubt."

"Lady Melbourne was quite obviously trying to steer him away from her daughter-in-law, Caroline Lamb," Lady Fitzwilliam asserted, "and who would blame her after the scandalous scenes that have taken place? I'm sure the stories have spread even to your part of the country, Sir George."

"They have indeed," Sir George said. "The young woman is, of course, quite mad and must be a terrible trial to her husband."

Miles looked amused. "What do you think of the passionate poet?" he asked Arabella.

"I think it's most interesting to see someone whose works you have read and enjoyed," she told him, quite obviously considering her words carefully before speaking, "and there is no question of the popularity of his *Childe Harold,* but I don't believe I have the slightest desire to meet him. Can you understand what I mean?''

''Completely,'' Miles told her, ''for though I have met him on a number of occasions and believe him to be quite brilliant, as a person he does not interest me. I was, however, most surprised to receive such a sensible answer to my rather facetious question.''

Something was puzzling Arabella, and she decided to see if Miles would give her the answer. ''Why did you choose to come here tonight?'' she asked. ''I noticed that you were not at all impressed with the performance of Lady Casterfield's brother.''

Miles looked startled and even a little guilty, but he quickly recovered himself as he recalled what George had told him on his return from the afternoon drive.

''I came because George wished to do so,'' he told her, hating to lie but considering it a necessity. ''He was interested in finding out what the young man was like, and I had no desire to go elsewhere alone.''

''He must have been extremely disappointed, then,'' Arabella suggested, ''for I studied his face also while the recitation was in progress and he looked as bored as I have ever seen him.''

Miles shrugged. ''I'm afraid that I was not so observant,'' he said, ''but I have no doubt I shall hear all about it when we get home.'' He paused. ''I was wondering if, perhaps, I could persuade you to go for a ride early tomorrow morning?''

Arabella's face suddenly came alive. ''I would be delighted, Miles,'' she said softly, her eyes shining. ''I enjoyed the ride so much the last time we went that I was hoping you might ask me again.''

When Miles smiled, his whole face seemed to soften. ''I'm glad to give you so much pleasure. I'll bring your mount around at about eight o'clock, if I may?''

''I will look forward to it,'' she promised. Suddenly she remembered his kiss, and her cheeks went a bright pink.

Miles looked pleased with her response, then he saw her flushed face and remembered what had happened the last time they had gone riding. He gave her what he hoped was a reassuring smile.

What he must do was to try to take her riding as frequently as possible these next two weeks, he decided. Though he did not at all regret that one slip, he must show her that he was still a gentleman and could be trusted to behave as one. If all went well, she should by then be so completely comfortable with him that an absence of a couple of weeks while the leg mended might not be such a bad thing, after all.

But what if it didn't happen that way? a voice inside him asked. What if she met someone else in his absence, someone like Richard? Then he remembered Ben and Dora and, of course, his uncle. With their help he would be able to keep himself informed of what Arabella was doing almost all of those two weeks, he realized. And if anything started to go wrong, he would not be completely out of touch, after all, for he was still in London, close by, and could do something—though what he could do while unable to walk he could not for the moment decide.

His instinct had been right, he thought, when he bought the young filly. It was an excellent way of getting her to himself for an hour or so. And though it appeared that they easily outrode his groom, that fellow knew he would be out of a job if he ever tried to keep up with them.

She had changed a great deal, of course, but fortunately her spirit had not been broken for he still saw glimpses of it when something caught her unawares. She had been betrayed by someone she thought she could trust, a friend of his, and he seriously doubted that she would let any man sweep her off her feet again. He had been able to penetrate the defenses she had erected only because he had taken it slowly, behaving as a friend and not a lover as yet. The defenses were still there, though, and it would take time to wear them down but it would be worth every ounce of effort.

First thing in the morning, after their ride, of course, he would get in touch with Tom Radcliff and make whatever arrangements were necessary. The sooner he got the thing over with, the better, for then he could court her like a whole man again. Right now, the only time he felt like his old self was when he was on horseback.

10

"I'll be going north in a few hours on some business," Miles said as he and Arabella cantered through the park.

She looked over at him in surprise. He must have known that he was going away, she thought. Why had he not said anything before now? Surely they were good-enough friends for him to have confided his plans before the very last minute?

It meant that he would not be at the card party tonight, and she would far rather play with him than anyone else. While she would miss him this evening, she knew she would miss even more their early-morning rides. Their friendship had grown gradually, at least on her side, into something she had, in fact, become concerned about. She did not want to experience the feelings about him that seemed to be growing stronger the more she saw of him. Perhaps, if he were away for a while, they would start to diminish. They must, for she could not let him become involved in the consequences of Richard's sins.

"Will you be gone long?" she asked, schooling her voice to sound merely polite.

"Probably a couple of weeks, or so," he said, then could not resist asking, "Will you miss me?"

She smiled. "Why, of course I will, Miles, for we meet so frequently at the homes of our friends that I cannot help but think we must have the same tastes."

Arabella knew that one of the reasons for this was because her aunt was long past the time when she enjoyed balls, and Miles' leg no doubt prevented him from dancing. But she had never seen the vast number of invitations her aunt received daily and did not know that a great many more were declined than accepted.

Miles thought for a moment that she was about to say something else, voice her suspicions perhaps about always meeting at the same parties, and he was considerably relieved when she did not.

"We always did," he said softly. "Don't you remember?"

"I remember a lot of things that I once tried very hard to forget, but couldn't," she said, her voice almost a whisper. "And then eventually the memories became like old friends and gave me comfort."

He wanted to ask her about those memories, but now was not the time to do so, for when he was so close to becoming normal again, he would rather wait until after it was over and he could offer her a whole man and not a cripple.

"I'm glad there was something for you to look back upon," he murmured softly, then he suddenly remembered something. "By the way, George told me that you had an unfortunate meeting in the park with my Cousin Audrey. I just want you to know that I went over to see her right away and set matters straight. She swore she had told no one of our betrothal six years ago and gave me her word that she will not spread old history about town now."

"I wish it had not been necessary," Arabella said with a sigh, "but I had completely forgotten about her until we came face to face in the park. I hope you were not too severe with her, for she has always thought a great deal of you and would be hurt by a scold."

"You're remembering how she used to stick to me like a leech when she visited for the summer," he said, smiling and shaking his head at the recollection. "What a little nuisance she was then. I thought sometimes that we'd never get a moment to ourselves, but she's different now that she has a husband and young son to take care of.''

Not as different as you think, Arabella said to herself, for she was quite sure after their unexpected meeting that his cousin still worshiped him and was being abnormally protective of him.

They were back at the entrance to the park and proceeded carefully through the streets to Hanover Square. The groom helped Arabella dismount, then she turned to Miles.

''I will miss you,'' she said, smiling up at him, ''for you have been very kind these last few weeks. Much, much nicer than I deserve, I know.''

Miles was embarrassed and cleared his throat loudly. ''Nonsense,'' he said gruffly. ''As far as I am concerned, you deserve only the best of everything. Just be a good girl while I'm gone.''

Arabella walked up the steps slowly. The last few words had such a familiar ring to them, for he had always said them to her in the old days when he was going anywhere. She had never thought to hear them again.

Suddenly she felt hungry, and she hurried into the breakfast room, where her aunt was sitting sipping the last dregs of her morning cup of coffee and avidly studying the latest edition of *The Times*. She was an extremely intelligent woman and liked to keep herself abreast of all that was going on both socially and politically.

After helping herself to a little of everything, Arabella took her place at the table.

Her aunt peered from behind the newspaper and smiled. ''Did you have a nice ride? I hope you made the most of it, for I understand it will be the last one for a couple of weeks or more.''

Arabella looked stunned. ''How did you know? Miles only told me a few minutes ago that he was going north this morning.''

Her aunt's eyes were twinkling. ''Is that the excuse he made? He's such a nice young man,'' she said appreciatively, ''but a little too self-conscious for my taste.''

Putting down her knife and fork, Arabella stared for a

moment at her aunt, then asked abruptly, "What do you mean by an excuse? Did Miles lie to me?"

Lady Fitzwilliam smiled and shook her head. "He told you a white lie, I believe, so that you would not worry about him, my love," she began. "You see, he is going into a hospital and that brilliant young doctor Sir George spoke of is going to operate on his leg again. He's going to try to ease the pain and perhaps even enable him to walk without that limp. George told me all about it last night, but you are not to let Miles know you have any idea what he is doing."

"But that's completely ridiculous," Arabella said crossly. "I could visit him and help him pass the time with a game of cards or something." She stabbed a piece of kidney with her fork and ate it hungrily.

"George tells me that Miles is very self-conscious about his disability and that he expects to be in considerable pain for some time after the surgery. He obviously feels that he must not inflict his own discomfort on other people, which I, for one, find very much to his credit," Lady Fitzwilliam pronounced.

"I suppose it is," Arabella agreed, "but he has always been very good to me and I would have liked to help if I could."

"Do you feel anything for him, my dear? He's certainly paid a lot of attention to you since you arrived in London, and I had hoped that something might come of it this time." The older lady looked at her niece with understanding eyes.

Arabella only wished she could tell her how she did feel and the reason she could not allow herself to become too involved with Miles, but she felt strongly that she had no right to bring anyone else into the path of the person who was sending the threatening letters.

"I like him very much, Aunt Gertrude" she said quietly, "as I did six years ago. I enjoy his company and feel gratified that he and his uncle have given us so much of their time and attention, but as for anything else . . ." She shrugged slightly. "I really don't know. It's too soon as yet."

"What do you think of Sir George?" Lady Fitzwilliam asked, a decided twinkle appearing in her eyes. "I realize that you have known him only since coming to London, for you did not socialize at all last year in the north country. However, I am sure you must have formed an opinion of him.''

Arabella glanced at her aunt, noting her slightly flushed face and her air of expectancy as she waited for a response.

"I do not, of course, know him very well, as you say, Aunt Gertrude, but in any dealings with him I have found him to be gentle and kind and very much aware of another person's feelings. Miles told me that when he joined the army and ignored his family obligations to his land, Sir George quietly took it upon himself to move to Warrington House and keep things running smoothly until Miles' return.'' Arabella saw the surprise on her aunt's face. "Did you think he was just living there at Miles' expense and doing nothing?''

"I did not know what to think, my dear, but that certainly puts him in another light. I suppose he then stayed on because he had become used to the place and also to be company for Miles?'' Lady Fitzwilliam suggested.

Arabella was nibbling on a piece of toast and just nodded. "I imagine so, and probably to help initially, for I heard that Miles was in much worse shape when he first came home than he is now,'' she said, then threw down her napkin and rose. "I'd best run upstairs and change out of this habit. Did you have any plans for the morning?''

"Only to write a few letters, my dear, and go through the invitations. Sir George is coming this afternoon to take me for a drive in the park, and he was hoping you might join us,'' Lady Fitzwilliam said, her eyebrows raised questioningly.

"Perhaps I will,'' Arabella started to say, and then wondered if she should stay home and let the two of them have some time to themselves. "I'll let you know when I come down for luncheon.''

Wouldn't it be wonderful, she thought as she went up the stairs, if the two older people decided to marry? Her aunt was a delightful lady, but she must be very lonely at times.

Arabella entered her bedchamber and Dora greeted her

cheerfully and helped her out of the riding habit; then, as she turned to take her arm out of the sleeve, Arabella saw the white envelope lying on the chest by her bed. She felt herself sway and might easily have fallen had the bedpost not been near enough for her to grasp.

"What is it, milady?" Dora asked, looking at her anxiously. "Shall I get the vinaigrette?"

"No, Dora," Arabella snapped. "I'm perfectly all right. I was just trying to wriggle my foot out of my boots and lost my balance."

"Yes, milady," Dora said while thinking to herself that there was nothing wrong with her ladyship's balance as a rule. Then she saw that her mistress was gazing at the envelope a footman had brought up earlier in the morning. "Why don't you just sit down for a minute," she said as she drew a chair forward, "and I'll bring you that letter that came for you earlier."

Arabella sank gratefully onto the chair, then reached out a trembling hand for the piece of paper. "That will be all for now, Dora," she said. "I'll ring for you in fifteen minutes or so, when I want you to help me dress."

As soon as the maid left, Arabella broke the seal and unfolded the paper. It was longer this time, but obviously from the same person and read: "YOU WILL SEE ME WHEN YOU LEAST EXPECT ME AND YOUR LAME LOVER WON'T BE ABLE TO HELP. YOU DON'T KNOW WHO I AM, BUT I KNOW WHO YOU ARE—AND WHAT YOU ARE."

Who could it be, and why was he trying to frighten her so? she asked herself. Was it possible he could know that Miles was not going to be seeing her for the next week or so?

Taking a firm hold of herself, she told her body to stop shaking like a leaf, and surprisingly, it obeyed. There was no point in brooding about it, she decided, for she had not the slightest notion of who the writer was. She rose and started to pace back and forth across the chamber, with the letter in her hand, then, realizing that this was not achieving anything either, she flung the letter down on the bed and rang for Dora.

"Don't you get any days off?" Arabella asked the girl as she helped her into a morning gown.

"I haven't taken any time off yet, milady, so I do have a half-day to come, but Mr. Dawson is very good and lets me go for a walk sometimes when you and her ladyship are out for the evening," the maid said with a shy smile.

"Well, that's good to hear," Arabella said, pleased that the elderly butler was kind to the staff under him. "You're happy here, then?"

"Oh, yes, milady, it's a good house to work in," she started to say, but noticed that Snowball was playing with what looked like her mistress's letter.

"Here, stop that, you little imp," the girl called as she bent down to take the letter from the cat. Then, as she retrieved it, her eyes lit on the three lines of bold letters printed across it. She gave a little gasp of surprise and dropped it quickly onto the escritoire. As though there had been no interruption, she continued, "Even the tweeny is well-looked-after."

"Why don't you take that half-day off tomorrow?" Arabella suggested, for, as she would not be seeing Miles, she did not feel quite so anxious to look her best. "The weather has been so lovely of late that I'd hate you to miss a fine day. One of the other maids can do anything I might need."

With profuse thanks, the maid left the chamber, but her delight in having some time off during the day did not make her forget her duty to Lord Cavendish. As soon as she could get out for a moment, she went to the stable and looked for Ben.

He wasn't expecting her, for he knew that his master would not be seeking any information about the ladies for a while, and she had to search before she saw him talking to another groom.

When he spotted her, he started to move almost casually in her direction; then, as he drew near, he muttered without looking up, " 'E's not looking fer owt fer a week or two. Is summat wrong?"

She nodded, glancing away.

He growled, "Be be'ind t'big coach in five minutes, then."

Dora slipped back into the kitchen to make sure she had not been missed, spoke with Cook for a moment, then went out as though going back to her mistress's bedchamber. She quickly doubled back and was at the specified place exactly on time.

"Wot is it?" Ben asked her, and she told him at once about the note that had arrived and what had been written on it.

"It came out of nowhere," Dora told him. "Nobody took it in or remembers anything about it until it was sitting on the hall table. And it's not the first time, either."

"Wot d'ye mean?" Ben asked, scowling. "Are ye saying ye've read others like it?"

Dora shook her head. "No, but one came before, with writing just like it on the outside, and no one knew how it had got here. Mr. Dawson said it was a real mystery."

"You'd better keep yer eyes open, Dora girl, 'cos it sounds a bit funny to me. Let me know if any more come, and 'ave a go at finding t'other one. She may 'ave kept it." He gave her a nod of approval, then slipped around one end of the coach as she went around the other.

With the arrival of another threatening letter, Arabella admitted to herself that she was frightened to go out alone, even accompanied by a maid, and she wondered if this persecution would ever end. Was the writer just trying to put her into a constant state of fear? Did he watch her, perhaps from the other side of the square, and sometimes follow her? And did he intend to approach her when the opportunity arose? If so, what might he do then?

As she and her aunt sipped tea and nibbled on biscuits and cheese after luncheon, Lady Fitzwilliam asked, "Are you going for a drive in that gown, my dear, or did you wish to run up to your bedchamber and change before Sir George arrives?"

Arabella chuckled. "You're afraid I might shame you in this old thing, I know. Actually, I decided to have a quiet afternoon writing letters and perhaps catching up on some reading. I'm ashamed to say that I have not yet finished Jane Austen's *Emma*, and I started it the day after I arrived in London.''

"Nonsense, child," Lady Fitzwilliam said firmly. "You need to get out into some fresh air, and you know quite well that Sir George will expect you to come for a ride. His invitation was to both of us.''

"Wouldn't you rather be alone with him, Aunt Gertrude?" Arabella asked softly. "You seem to enjoy his company very much, and—''

"I do enjoy Sir George's company," Lady Fitzwilliam firmly interrupted, "but I'm not yet ready for the *ton* to link our names together, as they might if I was seen too frequently alone with him. Tongues are quick to wag in this town, and I've not built up a good reputation here to lose it for the sake of an afternoon's drive.''

Arabella had not thought of that and was somewhat relieved to have a good excuse to accompany them. Without further argument she ran upstairs and changed into a more suitable gown, joining the two older people in the drawing room for a few minutes before they all got into the carriage and set out for the park.

As they circled the square, Arabella looked intently at every person who appeared to be loitering. She did not even glance at the tall, slim gentleman, dressed in the style of an upper-class servant, who walked briskly along, swinging his cane, and crossed New Bond Street just ahead of their carriage. Alex Galbraith did more than glance at her, however, and he noted with considerable satisfaction that she seemed more interested in the people on the street than in her companions.

"I told Arabella the truth about Miles, as you suggested," Lady Fitzwilliam said to Sir George, "and I believe she has a few questions you might be able to answer.''

He smiled at the younger woman. "By all means ask, my dear, and I'll tell you what I can," he assured her.

"Why did Miles lie to me about it?" she asked forthrightly.

"I had thought us to be good friends at this point and cannot think why he did not tell me the truth."

Sir George took his eyes off the road ahead for a moment and glanced at Arabella's hurt expression. "I believe at this point you are once again a little more than just good friends, and that is probably why he didn't want you to feel you must visit him. Also, I am sure, he would not like you to see him looking anything except at his best."

Arabella gave what sounded like a genteel snort. "Stubborn pride," she said in an exasperated tone, then asked, "Is there any danger in reopening the wound, Sir George?"

He shook his head. "None that I know of, my dear. It will be very painful, of course, but nothing like the last time, when the hospitals were filled with wounded soldiers, many of whom had not the slightest chance of survival. Conditions then were a disgrace, but this time he'll be in a separate wing, and he's every faith that this young doctor will succeed."

"I'm glad," Arabella said with a smile. "When he is finally allowed home, do you think I will be able to come and see him?"

"I really can't say," Sir George said gently, pleased that the girl seemed so concerned, "but I promise to give you bulletins on his progress."

They had now entered the park and Lady Fitzwilliam leaned forward. "Isn't that Lady Casterfield, George?" she asked. "Please stop, for I must tell her once again how very much we enjoyed her reception the other evening."

Sir George dutifully pulled over to the other carriage and the two ladies greeted each other as though they had not met in years. An afternoon drive in the park was every bit as much of a social event as the paying of calls, and Sir George smiled benevolently on the ladies, enjoying the idle chatter just as much as they did.

In fact, he had forgotten how enjoyable the Season really was, particularly when one had no need to become involved in the marriage mart. He had spent a lot of years in the north and had not missed it, for he had plenty to do on Miles' estate, but now he was glad he'd insisted on joining his nephew.

If the rascal persisted in recuperating without the aid of the ladies, however, he'd have to spend more time at home himself once the lad was home, giving him a game of chess or piquet, and that would not quite fit in with his own plans. Gertrude Fitzwilliam was as fine-looking a woman as he'd ever met, and he had no wish to stop seeing her. He'd have to talk Miles into letting Arabella know what he'd been about, so that the ladies could come to visit.

In fact, that was just the answer, for, married before to a cardplayer, Arabella had to be quite adept at cards herself and could give Miles a worthwhile game, he decided.

In this he was, however, quite wrong, for Arabella was an indifferent cardplayer, but she could hold her own at chess.

They were now pulled alongside Lady Winterford's carriage and the ladies were talking twenty to the dozen. Out of the corner of his eye Sir George noticed someone staring at the carriage. The man was standing under a tree, and come to think of it, he'd been doing just the same thing farther back, when they were talking with Lady Casterfield.

There was something familiar about the man, but Sir George didn't know quite what. Then he chuckled to himself. The man was a butler, of course, and probably worked at the home of one of his acquaintances. The thing was, one saw the same kind of clothes on all of them but never noticed their faces. He shrugged. It was a warm day and the fellow was probably walking awhile, then standing under some trees to get a bit of shade. Couldn't blame him for that.

11

Arabella struggled to keep from awakening, for the delightful dream she had been having was already trying to slip away, and she wanted to recapture at least a fragment of it. Miles had been in the dream, she knew, and there had been something different about him. She smiled, for now she recalled that he had not been lame, but which one was it, the Miles she had known long ago or the Miles of today, after the operation?

There had been something else, and it was teasing her memory, almost coming back, then escaping again. She closed her eyes once more, but all she saw was Dawson, Aunt Gertrude's butler. What on earth was he doing in her dream?

After knocking lightly on the door, Dora entered and Arabella noticed at once that there was an unusual air of concealed excitement about her.

Sipping the hot chocolate the maid had brought, Arabella watched her fling open the curtains and smile as the sun poured into the room. Then the maid almost skipped across to the dresser, picked up the water jug, and a moment later disappeared through the door.

Filled with curiosity, Arabella continued to sip the hot

drink but could contain herself no longer when the girl returned carrying the steaming jug of water, a broad smile on her face.

"It's nice to see you so happy first thing on a morning, Dora," she told the maid. "Did something special happen?"

"Oh, milady," the girl said, quite obviously eager to talk about it, "when Mr. Dawson let me go out for some air last night, I met the most handsome gent. And so proper, he was."

Arabella smiled as she got out of bed and let Dora put a robe around her shoulders. She liked to think that the girl was happy.

"He told me he's a footman at the Prince's house on Pall Mall, and he said they're all excited about Princess Charlotte's wedding," the maid went on. "He said that he might be able to get me in to see it if I could get that day off."

"Then we'll have to make sure that you do," Arabella said firmly as she dried her face on a soft towel. "You mustn't miss such an opportunity. Years from now, you'll be able to tell your children and grandchildren all about it. And I must say I envy you the chance. But how is he going to get you inside?"

Dora seated her mistress before the dressing table and began to unbraid her hair.

"He says it's easy. He's worked there for a long time, so he got the job of picking out the extra staff they're taking on for the day," she explained between sweeps of the brush.

"What is his name?" Arabella asked.

"Godfrey, milady," the maid told her, "and he told me as how the wedding is going to be in the Crimson Drawing Room and there'll be only fifty guests besides the Prince's family." She giggled. "He said he might be able to hide me inside before the wedding begins, so as I can see it all."

"But that's wonderful, Dora," Arabella exclaimed. "You'd be one of the few people in the whole of London to see the wedding. How I wish that I were in your place, for I've never seen a single member of the royal family."

"What a shame! You've never been presented, then,

milady?'' The girl's eyes were round with surprise as she helped her mistress into a morning gown.

"Not yet, but I shall be before the end of the Season,'' Arabella told her, then asked. "When are you meeting this young man again?''

"This afternoon.'' Dora was beaming. "He's taking me out on my half-day off,'' she said as she tied and concealed the drawstring on the gown, then pulled at the small sleeves to puff them out.

Arabella looked at herself in the pier glass, turning around and peeking over her shoulder to be sure the back looked equally good. "Well, if you want to see the wedding, you'd better mind you don't keep him waiting,'' she admonished. "I'll need you for a few minutes before luncheon, then you're free until it's time to help me undress for dinner.''

Getting away so early meant that Dora would have time to make herself look her best before meeting Godfrey. She was almost bursting with pride at just the idea of seeing such an occasion, and as soon as her mistress left the room, she set to with a will, tidying it up a bit, then gathering up all the garments that needed ironing or repair. As she left the room, the chambermaid hurried in to take care of everything else.

Except for a few minutes before luncheon, Arabella did not see the maid again until she needed help to dress for dinner, and then the girl was even more excited.

"You look as though you had an enjoyable afternoon,'' Arabella said with a smile. "I hope everything is arranged, for the wedding is less than a week away.''

Dora took down the pale-lavender gown that her mistress was to wear this evening, inspecting it carefully to be sure that it had not been creased since she had ironed it earlier in the day. Then with a satisfied smile she laid it upon the bed and turned to Arabella.

"I hope you won't take it amiss, milady,'' she began, excited but nervous. "But if you'd really like to see the wedding, too, Godfrey said as he could arrange to get you in.''

"That's very kind of him, but I'm afraid that, much as I would love to see it, I could hardly do so dressed as a servant. Were I found out, I could never show my face in London again," Arabella said regretfully.

"Oh, no, milady, that's not what he meant for you," Dora said, quite shocked. "He knows of a lord who has been invited and his lady can't attend. Godfrey said that it would look real bad if a seat was empty, so they want a lady just to sit with him during the service."

Arabella frowned. "Why would it look bad, Dora? I would think no one would notice in the excitement."

Looking very important, Dora explained. "Except for the family, there's only fifty people been invited, so an empty seat would make it look as though someone didn't want to come, and Godfrey says that'd be an insult to the Prince. Do you see?"

"Well, I suppose it would stand out, but why doesn't this lord ask someone he knows to go with him?" Arabella asked.

"Because if he asked one lady, then all the others he knows would be jealous, don't you see, milady?" Dora asked. "Godfrey said that if you want to go, he must know by tonight, or he'll have to look for someone else. You see he's promised the lord he'll take care of it. There'll not be any questions asked as to who you are, for you'll not be staying for the reception. It's just for the wedding itself."

Arabella was beginning to think what fun it would be to see the ceremony. And if this Godfrey was on hand to whisk her away afterward, how could anything go wrong?

"But how would I get there?" she asked. "I would not like to go to some strange man's house and drive with him in his carriage."

Dora smiled broadly, for she realized her mistress had finally understood how easy it would all be. "Godfrey's got it all worked out," she said proudly. "We'd leave here together and take a hackney to Warwick Street. It's the back way to Carlton House, but he says we'd never get through the crowds that'll be in front all day long. He'll be waiting for us there and take us inside."

Arabella still looked a little dubious. "What time are we to be there?" she asked.

"He said we'd best be there by seven o'clock, and to tell you everybody'd be wearing their finest gowns and jewels, and you'd best cover yourself up in a big cloak till you go inside, so no one can see." The maid smiled. "He's so clever, milady. He thought of everything, didn't he?"

It was a risk, Arabella knew, but she finally decided it was one worth taking. "All right," she said. "I'll do it. You can thank your young man for me when you see him, and tell him I appreciate his efforts on my behalf. Also, ask him how I will get away after the wedding, for that's even more important."

Suddenly Arabella was excited also. It was something she would never forget, to be one of the fifty people to see a future queen of England marry her prince.

There was, of course, always the chance that she might see someone who knew her, but this was a remote one for, aside from her aunt, she rarely met anyone of the rank the fifty guests were bound to be.

And then there was the question of what she would wear. Something very rich-looking was called for, but she did not want to wear anything that would make her stand out too much. The only one of her gowns that answered the description was a cream brocade embroidered with very delicate leaves in various shades of green. It had a high waist and puffed sleeves, and a big square neckline that certainly called for jewelry. Here Godfrey would be quite disappointed if he knew anything about stones, for, except for the sapphire set, all but one of the necklaces she possessed had been bought by Richard and were very beautiful imitations.

She was wearing her other good necklace tonight, a string of pearls with a single pear-shaped amethyst in the center. It had been a sort of welcome back gift from her father and she wore it as often as she could. Tonight it looked particularly well with her lavender gown.

All of a sudden she realized that she had been daydreaming and that her aunt would be wondering where she was, so she quickly snatched up a beaded reticule and a lace shawl and hurried downstairs.

"How pretty you look in that color, my dear," Lady Fitzwilliam told her as she entered the drawing room. "I forgot to tell you that your papa is dining in tonight and accompanying us to Vauxhall Gardens. He feels that Sir George cannot possibly protect two ladies at once in such a dangerous place."

Although she heard the laughter in her aunt's voice, Arabella was much relieved to have two men escort them, for she had heard of strange things happening in some of Vauxhall's secluded walks. The letters were making her nervous enough already, and she knew she would be looking over her shoulder too much of the time to really enjoy herself. But her aunt had been so eager to take her there that she simply could not refuse.

"What time is Sir George coming for us?" she asked her aunt. She was hoping to get him on her own for a few minutes to find out if Miles' operation had been a success and to ask if she might visit, though she thought she already knew what the answer to that would be.

"He'll be here at any moment," Lady Fitzwilliam said with a pleased smile, "for I invited him to have dinner with us instead of eating home alone this evening. He'll send his coach back and we'll go in mine, however, and then drop him at Miles' house on our return. Don't worry, you'll have plenty of opportunity to ask how Miles is going along, my love."

They both turned at the sound of Lord Darnley's voice in the hall and a moment later he entered the room.

He went over to where Arabella was sitting sipping her sherry and bent down to kiss her on the cheek. "This is indeed a pleasure, my dear," he said warmly. "You've been so busy with your young man that I've not seen much of you lately. And that's how it should be," he hastened to add as he observed a guilty flush on his daughter's cheek, "just so long as I know you're here and enjoying yourself is enough for me. I must say you look lovelier than ever."

"Thank you, Papa," Arabella said softly. "It's because

I'm so happy to be here with my family again. And I'm so glad you're coming with us tonight.''

Lord Darnley chuckled. "When I heard where you were going, I decided that Sir George would have his hands full just keeping your aunt out of trouble without watching you also," he said. "That sounds like him now."

He was right, for a moment later Sir George entered the room. He went directly over to Lady Fitzwilliam, bowed low over her hand, and then approached Arabella.

"You must be eager to hear how Miles is, my dear," he said gently, "and I have good news. I saw him earlier today and I'm happy to tell you that the operation was a success. I met the young doctor in whom he has so much faith, and I was extremely impressed. Miles is in the best of hands, and all he has to do now is to rest and follow instructions."

Arabella did not even notice her own huge sigh of relief, nor had she any idea how radiant her smile was, but her father missed neither of these obvious expressions of feeling for Miles. This time everything was going to work out right, he decided.

Sir George's good news set the mood for the evening, and dinner was a happy affair, with much laughter, good wine, and excellent food. Immediately they were finished, the coach was brought around and they set out for what promised to be a delightful evening's entertainment with fireworks, a band, and some light refreshments.

None of them had any idea that they carried an extra passenger, however, for as the carriage started out a dark figure jumped lightly onto the back, then settled himself down for a rather bumpy ride. Ben was acting on his own this time, for his master was not in a position to give him instructions. He had heard, from Dora, where they were going this evening and had decided to stay close to Lady Arabella, for he had not liked the tone of that anonymous letter one bit. He could think of no better place for an attack on a lady than a dark walkway in Vauxhall Gardens, if that was what the writer had in mind.

"As Arabella has never been to Vauxhall before," Sir George said, "we thought we might alight from the carriage on this side of the Thames, as we always used to, and cross over to the gardens by boat. The carriage will cross by the new Regent's Bridge and be waiting to take us back that way when we are ready to leave."

"What an excellent idea," Lady Fitzwilliam exclaimed. "I clearly recall attending the grand fete marking Wellington's victory at Vitoria. I was a little afraid of crossing by boat because of the crush, so we started out more than an hour before we need have done normally and went by Westminster Bridge. Can you believe that it took almost three hours to get from the bridge to the gardens?"

"It must have been a little frightening," Arabella said, "for it would have been so easy for someone to rob stationary carriages. Did you find it worthwhile when you finally arrived there?"

"Of course it was. All the royal dukes were there, you know, and the gardens were illuminated more brightly than I have ever seen them," Lady Fitzwilliam told them, realizing that none of the others was in London at that time. "There were three displays of fireworks, bands were playing everywhere, and then the evening ended with dancing."

"Did Miles take part in the Battle of Vitoria?" Arabella asked Sir George.

"Yes, Miles was there. In fact, it was because of Vitoria that he was promoted to colonel," he said with a smile. "He told me that after the battle he and his men helped confiscate the art treasures, supplies, and a great deal of currency that King Joseph had taken with him but been forced to abandon on his flight toward the French border."

There was no time for Arabella to question him further, for they had stopped. The gentlemen alighted first, then assisted the ladies out of the carriage and down the Mill Bank stairs to where several boats waited.

The lights of the gardens were clearly visible on the other side, and it made such a delightful way to start the evening's entertainment that Arabella almost regretted they would not be returning that way, but would be driving over the cast-iron bridge that loomed above them on their right.

She entered the gardens on her father's arm, followed by

her aunt and Sir George, and she gasped at the fairylike beauty stretching before her down the Grand Walk along which they strolled until they reached the supper box that had been reserved for them.

She would not have noticed Ben, even had she seen him pass their box and stand a little to one side in a particularly shady spot, for she did not know one of her aunt's grooms from another and, in any case, he was dressed this evening in the Sunday best clothes of a workingman.

"I ordered claret first," Sir George told them, "for the Vauxhall punch or the arrack that are so popular here are also much too potent, I believe, for the ladies."

Lord Darnley nodded his agreement. "I think we might sit here watching the people passing for a while, then take the ladies closer when the fireworks begin."

Arabella touched her aunt's arm. "Just look at that lady wearing a mask," she said in shocked tones. "I don't wonder she does not wish to be recognized when she's so scantily clad."

"You'll see much worse than that before the night's out, my dear," Lady Fitzwilliam told her as she glanced at the light-skirt who was making her way slowly, with exaggeratedly swaying hips, toward the Dark Walk. "Just be sure that you stay on your father's arm when we leave this box."

Refreshments had arrived and soon they were nibbling on biscuits topped with slivers of ham and chicken, and sipping the wine.

"It's a pity there will not be a balloon ascension this evening, Arabella," her father said, "for I'm sure you would have found it most interesting."

"She'll see one another time," Lady Fitzwilliam put in, "by daylight, if possible, for it's far more interesting to watch all the preparations before the thing actually goes up. Personally, at night I'd much rather watch a good firework display, and tonight's promises to be just that."

"They'll be starting soon, I think," Sir George said. "As soon as we finish eating, it might be a good idea to stroll over there and get a good position. The box is ours for the evening, so we can always come back later and have a little more to eat if we wish."

Shortly afterward, they left the box and strolled over to where, by past experience, they knew they could get the best view of the display. A hissing sound heralded the first of a series of rockets that flew high into the air and, after a loud bang, sent out a dazzling display of brightly colored stars.

As one after another went up, Arabella gasped with delight, for it was even more beautiful than anything she had imagined. She stepped back to get a better view of one particularly lovely rainbow display, completely forgetting that she was no longer holding her father's arm.

Suddenly, her own arm was grasped from behind and she found herself being dragged backward toward a wooded area. She screamed but at that moment the fireworks were making so much noise that her voice could not be heard above the loud bangs.

She was now at the far edge of the crowd of people, but most of them were looking up at the sky and did not notice anything unusual happening. Struggle as she may, she could not free herself from the powerful hand that had her arm in such a grasp that it had begun to go numb. One of her slippers had come off and her heel was scraping painfully on the rough ground.

Then, all at once, she heard a gruff voice say, "Oh no you don't," and she was free, but had fallen flat on her back. She heard the sounds of a scuffle going on behind her and tried to sit up, then two strong hands grasped her under the arms and set her upon her feet.

"Are you all right, miss?" a gruff voice asked her, and she tried to see who her rescuer was, but after a quick glance at her he had bent down to try to put the missing slipper back onto her foot.

"Arabella," Lady Fitzwilliam's voice could just be heard between the bangs of rockets. "What happened? I told you to—"

"Leave her alone for now, Gertrude," Lord Darnley said, reaching his daughter's side first and turning toward the man who had obviously been helping her, but who had suddenly disappeared into the crowd. "Are you all right, my dear?"

"I think so," Arabella said, rubbing her sore arm. "I don't really know what happened. One minute I was looking up watching the fireworks, and the next one I was being pulled away. I never even saw who was doing it."

"Well, never mind, as long as you're all right now," he said, then called, "George, I think we'd best get her back to the box and let her sit down awhile. You and Gertrude lead the way, if you will."

Aside from a badly bruised arm and a scraped heel, Arabella seemed none the worse for her "accident," as she preferred to call it for now, and when she had drunk another glass of claret, she began to feel as though she had dreamed the whole incident. As she rested, she watched the remaining fireworks from the box; and then, with her aunt on one side of her and her father on the other, she limped out of Vauxhall Gardens and into the waiting carriage.

She did not even notice when they crossed Regent's Bridge, but was grateful when they reached Hanover Square and was hurried up to her bedchamber, for her head had started to ache unbearably.

Between Dora and her aunt, she was quickly undressed, some salve was put on her heel, and she was given a sedative that put her to sleep within a few minutes.

12

It was almost ten o'clock in the morning when Lady Fitzwilliam went to her niece's bedchamber, and even then she hesitated at the door before tapping lightly upon it and opening it just a crack. The girl, surely, had every right to stay in bed the whole day if she wished after that dreadful incident of the previous night, but she just wanted to make sure she was all right.

As her eyes moved from one side of the room to the other, she pushed the door wider open until she was standing there gazing at the completely empty room. If she had not known better, she would have thought that her niece had never slept there at all, for even the bed had already been made and the room put in order.

Turning quickly, she hurried downstairs in time to join Arabella just as she was finishing her breakfast.

"My dear," Lady Fitzwilliam asked her gently, "are you sure that you should be up and around so soon after what happened last night?" She kissed the girl's cheek and looked closely to see if there were any signs of ill effect.

"I'm not too sure what really did happen last night, Aunt Gertrude. I think I became so excited on seeing some of those exploding starbursts that I stepped backward and automatically withdrew my hand from Papa's arm. I suppose I must have appeared to be standing alone and some drunk decided I was one of those dreadful women who were looking for men.''

"How could anyone possibly think that of you, my dear?'' Lady Fitzwilliam said crossly. "You were certainly not dressed like one of those women, but then I suppose that when some men are in their cups, they are incapable of telling the difference. Do you recall what he looked like?''

Arabella shook her head. "I have really no idea, for I never saw him. You see, he grabbed my arm from behind and then just kept on walking and pulling me backward with him.''

Lady Fitzwilliam shuddered. "What a good thing it was that the other nice little man came along just at that moment. I would have liked to reward him, but he disappeared as soon as we came onto the scene.''

"If I can, I mean to forget all about it now," Arabella said firmly. "You had warned me about holding Papa's arm, and in the future I shall make sure I take more notice of your good advice.'' While her aunt helped herself to some breakfast, Arabella went on, "Do you know if any of your friends have been included among the fifty of Princess Charlotte's wedding guests?''

"Not one, to my knowledge,'' Lady Fitzwilliam said as she took her place at the table and reached for some toast. "I might very well have been, were my husband still alive, but the honor would decidedly not be worth having to put up with him again.''

"It's only a few days away, isn't it?'' Arabella asked, knowing full well when it was but trying to sound casual.

"Two days, to be exact,'' Aunt Gertrude stated. "And I'll be glad when they're married and off on their wedding trip so that the London streets will be a little less crowded. You'd think that half of England had come up to the city to try to catch a glimpse of the young couple.''

"The people seem to have taken a liking to Prince Leopold. I hear that crowds have come to gape at him and that they shout for him to come out onto the balcony of Clarence House,'' Arabella remarked. "I keep wondering how he will possibly get through all those people when he comes from there to Carlton House on the day of the wedding.''

Lady Fitzwilliam smiled. ''I believe that Prince William, as his host, will make sure he gets there in one piece, if that's what you're worried about, my dear. But I think that what the common people like about the bridegroom is the plainness of his dress and his carriage, and that will change, I am sure, when he has the princess's dowry to spend upon himself.''

Arabella could not help thinking how cynical her aunt sounded, and hoped that her views on marriage might change as she got to know Sir George better. She had already decided that it would be an ideal match and intended to do her very best to promote it.

She was glad that it was to be an evening wedding, for it would have been quite difficult for her to get away during the day. The incident last night had helped her in one way, for though she was still tired and ached a little, she determined to do everything they had planned and more, so that she would be able to cry off on the evening of the wedding by saying she had overdone and must have an early night.

At Miles Cavendish's residence, a completely different scene was taking place.

The surgery had been successful, but Miles was still confined to his bed in order to give the leg a chance to heal. He was sitting up having breakfast from a bed tray when his man, Vernon, came in to tell him that Ben was asking to see him.

''Send him up right away,'' Miles ordered as his thoughts immediately flew to Arabella. He knew that she had been going to Vauxhall Gardens last night, with her father and George Wetherby, but he had not seen George as yet this morning.

Ben took his cap off as he entered the chamber and came over to the man who had been his master and friend for a number of years.

''It's good to see you, Ben,'' Miles said, smiling. ''Or it is as long as you're not bringing me any bad news. Sit down, can't you, for I despise having to twist my neck to look up at you.''

Ben reached for a seat and sat a little awkwardly by the side of the bed. He cleared his throat. "It's like this, milord," he began, "and I 'ate telling you when you're laid up like this, but it looks as though someone's threatening to do Lady Arabella an injury.''

Miles gave such an awkward start that his coffee spilled over onto the tray. Vernon came over immediately to remove it to a side table and glared at Ben, who ignored him and went on.

"Dora told me about a letter that came t'other day, and I 'ad 'er write it down to show you. I told 'er to look for others, and she found 'em an' copied 'em as well.'' He passed the pieces of paper to his employer and friend.

"It's a pity blackmailers don't date their letters," Miles remarked dryly, "that is, of course, if blackmail is his objective. Do you know how they came into her possession?''

Ben shook his head. "They seem t'just appear out of thin air. One of 'em was found right after that party you were at, to introduce 'er ladyship to t'marchioness's friends.''

"And he has to be in London watching her movements, or he would not know about me," Miles murmured.

Ben had a feeling that his master had not yet heard what happened last night, or he'd not be so calm. "Did Sir George tell ye that she was attacked last night, sir?'' he asked.

It was a very good thing that the tray had been removed from the bed altogether, or there might easily have been coffee on the ceiling. Miles jumped as though he meant to leap out of bed, then settled back with a groan.

He shook his head, then said, "I assume you were there, so you'd best tell me all about it.''

Ben carefully cleared his throat. "When I 'eard that it was Vauxhall Gardens they were goin' to, I didn't like t'sound of it, so I put on me Sunday best, 'opped on t'back of t'carriage, an' went along with 'em. They didn't notice me at all, of course, for t'ladies don't see me enough to remember me face.

"I follered 'em in t'next boat over t'river and stood by

their box while they ate. Then when they got up to go see t'fireworks I tagged along a bit be'ind 'em. I noticed this feller afore 'e tried anythin', and I'd know 'im again if I saw 'im. The young lady was 'oldin' 'er pa's arm all t'time until she got excited an' forgot." Ben looked grim as he went on. " 'E was there in a minute, grabbin' 'er arm and draggin' 'er backward to t'woods. I socked 'im one 'e'll not forget in a 'urry, but 'e got away while I was seeing to t'young lady," he said regretfully.

"Didn't her father or anyone realize what was happening?" Miles asked angrily.

"No, sir, no one was takin' any notice. They were all lookin' up at t'fireworks. If I 'adn't been there, 'e'd 'ave got clean away with 'er. She must 'ave been so frightened she couldn't scream, or else t'bangs drowned 'er out."

Miles tapped the copies of the letters. "Do you think it was this man, Ben, or could it have been just some drunken fool looking for some fun with her?"

"I couldn't rightly say, sir," Ben began, a worried expression on his face. "If it was 'im, then 'ow did 'e know they were goin' to be there? With you laid up like this, I wouldn't 'ave known if Dora 'adn't mentioned it in passin' like."

"Describe him to me," Miles instructed, and Ben closed his eyes as if to get a better image of the man.

"About five ten or eleven," he began, "thirty or so, and not in bad shape. Even if I 'adn't noticed 'im before, I'd 'ave got a good look, for 'e was facin' me and comin' my way, draggin' 'er along backward, as I said. 'E was clean-shaven, and 'ad the look of a gentleman with 'is long nose and thin lips."

"How was he dressed?" Miles asked abruptly.

"Just like any gent, sir. 'E might 'ave been any one of your friends with 'is top 'at, gloves, and cane," Ben asserted, then an idea struck him. "Come to think of it, sir, 'e probably was one of your sort, for 'e never looked at me once, though I was near enough for 'im to see me. An' 'e didn't expect it at all when I planted 'im a facer."

"Which could still mean that he was a drunk out to have

a little fun with a lady,'' Miles remarked, frowning.

Ben shook his head slowly. "I don't think so, sir. 'E wasn't lookin' for just a woman; 'e was watchin' 'er for fifteen minutes or more before she let go 'er pa's arm. It was almost as if 'e was just waitin' till she did."

Miles glanced down to where his game leg made a bump in the covers and he groaned in frustration. "You'd best tell Dora to let you know everywhere Lady Arabella is going, and tag along somehow, for I can't depend on Sir George to be there all the time. I am sure, however, that when I tell him of this, he will keep a close watch when he's with her from now on."

As though the mention of his name conjured him up, Sir George entered the bedchamber, and Ben immediately vacated his seat.

"Sit down, Ben," he said breezily. "I won't be a minute. I just wanted to find out how this young nephew of mine is getting along. Not too well, I should say, just by the scowl on his face."

"Ben has been telling me of the attack on Arabella last night," Miles said quietly, nodding to Ben to stay. "Did you see the man who did it, George?"

"No. I'm afraid I knew nothing about it until it was all over. I imagine it was one of those hooligans who goes about the gardens looking for girls to take into the Dark Walk. She was frightened, but not hurt badly, thank goodness," Sir George said with relief, then he realized what Miles had said and he turned and looked at Ben with a puzzled expression on his face.

"Was it you, by any chance, who rescued her, Ben?" he asked, and when Ben nodded, he turned back to Miles. "Were you expecting something to happen, Miles? Why didn't you let me know?"

"I wasn't expecting anything, but Ben was," Miles told him, holding out the letters. "Just take a look at these."

There was a silence while Sir George read the letters then handed them back to Miles. "I assume this is more of Dora's work and Arabella doesn't know you have these. What can I do to help?"

"Watch over her for me when you're out anywhere. We still can't be sure if it was the writer who attacked her. Ben will give you a description of the man he foiled last night, and—"

He was interrupted by a knock on the door. A maid came in to say that Dr. Radcliff was here.

Without a word, Sir George took Ben's arm and steered him out of the bedchamber and into the study, to give privacy to the tall young doctor who followed closely on the heels of the maid.

"How's everything going?" Dr. Radcliff asked when he and Miles were alone. "No problems, I hope?"

"Not as far as the leg is concerned, Tom, but I wish now that I'd either had it taken care of earlier or else waited a little longer," Miles grunted. "I'm not used to feeling so helpless."

"You're not considering breaking your word, I hope?" Radcliff's boyish looking face was stern.

Miles shook his head. "In my present condition I'd not be any use at all. The leg is doing fine, though," he assured the good doctor.

"You mean you're not having any pain at all, Miles?" Radcliff asked with a frown. "That's unusual."

Miles smiled. "I think it's a matter of comparisons, Tom. When measured against what I've been feeling these last months, my leg is very comfortable."

"Wait until next week when I start you on exercises," Radcliff said with a grin as he pulled back the covers. "I'll just take a look."

A half-hour later, the doctor left feeling very pleased with his work, and five minutes after that Miles took a well-earned nap. Sir George Wetherby and Ben had worked out a plan by which to protect Arabella and had promised to keep Miles abreast of everything as it occurred.

Ben hastened back to the Fitzwilliam stables before the head groom started to look for him.

As Arabella went from one activity to another, she feared that she really might tire herself to a point where she could not move another inch by evening, for it seemed that most of her aunt's friends were either giving or attending parties celebrating Princess Charlotte's wedding.

They returned from one of these in the late afternoon, taking three times as long to reach Hanover Square as they would normally have done, and as she stepped from the carriage, Arabella staggered a little. She reached to grasp a footman's arm and almost pulled the poor man over in her desire to appear truly exhausted.

"My dear, are you feeling all right?" Aunt Gertrude asked anxiously, placing an arm around her niece's waist. "I knew you were doing too much too soon after that awful incident. One of you hurry and get Dora to come help her mistress up the stairs," she called to her footmen.

"I'll be all right, truly I will," Arabella said weakly, hoping her aunt would not herself collapse under the weight she was placing upon her.

"You're going right to bed, my girl, and I'll see that you take something to make you sleep till morning," Lady Fitzwilliam said firmly. "I'll make apologies for you at Lady Gilbert's early reception, and also at the Rutherfords' dinner party, but Sir George is coming at six o'clock, so I may not have time to look in on you before I leave."

A few moments later, Arabella found herself tucked into bed with Dora appointed to watch over her all evening in case she woke and needed something. She had not, of course, taken the draft to make her sleep but had assigned it to the chamber pot as soon as her aunt had left the room.

Dora quickly helped her mistress into her undergarments so that all she had to do as soon as Lady Fitzwilliam left with Sir George was to slip into the cream brocade gown, have her hair dressed, and put on the fake necklace.

They both heard Lady Fitzwilliam go down the stairs and greet Sir George, then Dora went quietly out into the hall and peered over the banister until she saw the two figures disappear into the waiting carriage.

Arabella had flung back the covers and leapt out of bed before Dora had scarcely come back into the room, then, not ten minutes later, the two of them crept stealthily down the back stairs and out into the kitchen garden.

"I do hope we can get a hackney, milady," Dora whispered. "I tried to get one of them to promise to wait for us, but he wouldn't hear of it."

With cloaks concealing their attire, they walked quickly across to Swallow Street, where there was a cab rank, and they were in luck, for there was not one but two hackneys waiting for hire. As they stepped into the first one, the maid gave the address and the driver started off at a steady pace. Arabella sighed with relief, for Swallow Street was usually pretty quiet at this hour of the night, and it ran right down to Piccadilly. If they had to, they could walk from there, but she would prefer to ride all the way if possible.

Now she was truly excited. Her tiredness earlier in the day had not all been pretense, for she had been so worried about getting away without anyone seeing them that she had tired herself out. The weariness had left her completely, however, and all she could think of now was that she was really on her way and could look forward to seeing history take place before her eyes. In the years ahead, Dora would not be the only one who could tell her children and grand-children that she was there when it happened.

They reached Piccadilly and turned left along it, moving more slowly now, and then to almost a crawl as they turned right into the Haymarket, which was crowded with people.

Once they were past Pall Mall, now just a solid mass of bodies, it quietened a little and the hackney was able to get over to the right and turn on Warwick Street. Halfway down, the street narrowed, and fearing he'd not be able to turn around, the driver told them it was as far as he could go.

After paying him, Dora stepped down and helped her mistress to alight. Then, holding hands, they walked along the dark, narrow street until they found themselves facing a courtyard at the side of Carlton House, but cut off from it by a high fence. A passage seemed to lead toward Pall Mall, but it was so dim that they could hardly see the outlines of the walls.

"Ah, there you are, Dora." The cultured voice seemed to echo in the narrow passageway, and Arabella felt herself jump with surprise. "And this is Lady Arabella Barton, I presume."

She should have insisted on meeting Dora's friend before coming here, Arabella realized, for now there seemed to be something almost sinister in the way this man, whose face she could not see in the dim light, addressed her.

"Why don't you just go up this passage, Dora?" the man who called himself Godfrey suggested. "One of the household maids is waiting at the other end for you, and she'll take you where you need to be. I have to explain to Lady Barton just what she must do once she gets inside."

He tried to take Arabella's arm, and mindful of what had happened a couple of nights before, she stepped quickly away from him, but as she did so, she felt a hand near her throat and the paste necklace broke as it was jerked away from her neck. Suddenly, she was grasped around the waist from behind and pulled away from Godfrey. A vaguely familiar figure stepped in front of her.

"You can do yer explainin' to this," Ben said, and there was the sound of a fist making hard contact with flesh and bone.

Realizing something was amiss, for there had been no maid waiting for her at the end of the passage, Dora had started back and was knocked to the ground as her friend, Godfrey, raced past her. Ben was hot on his heels and tried to jump over the maid just as she was attempting to get to her feet, and the pair of them landed in a heap on the ground. Cursing loudly, Ben took off once more along the passage, but Godfrey had disappeared long ago into the crowd of Londoners waiting to see the bride and her groom.

With an expression of disgust more than obvious on his face, Ben went back to where Lady Arabella and Dora now waited.

Suddenly, Arabella realized it was the same man who had rescued her previously, but before she could get a word out, Dora said quietly, "This is Ben, milady, one of her ladyship's grooms. He must have followed us when we left Hanover Square.''

"An' lucky for t'pair of you that I did,'' Ben growled. ''There's a 'ackney waitin' for us just at the end 'ere. Come on and I'll get ye back 'ome.''

Without a word, Arabella went over to the cab and stepped inside, and a very much subdued Dora joined her. Ben got up beside the driver and directed him around to the back of Lady Fitzwilliam's house.

He took care of the cabdriver, then led them toward the back door, and it was not until they were almost there that anyone spoke. Then Arabella said to Ben, ''It was the same man who attacked me in Vauxhall Gardens, wasn't it?''

He looked surprised, for he hadn't thought that she had noticed him last time. ''Yes, milady, it was 'im all right,'' he replied, then he opened the door and made sure that no one was around before beckoning for them to go ahead. As soon as they were inside, Dora led the way up the back stairs and they were fortunate enough to reach Arabella's chamber without meeting anyone.

Dora opened her mouth several times to try to say something, but the expression on Lady Arabella's face stopped her. She could feel her mistress start to tremble as she undressed her and helped her on with her night rail; she wanted to tell her how sorry she was for her mistake, but knew this was not the time. ''Is there anything else I can do for you, milady? Get you a warm brick for your bed, perhaps?'' she asked.

Arabella just looked at her blankly and shook her head, then her eyes fell on the cream brocade gown. ''Before you go, you can put that gown to the very back of the armoire. I don't think I ever want to see it again,'' she said.

Once the girl did as she asked and then left the chamber, Arabella got into bed and turned on her side, shuddering uncontrollably now. Some time later the shudders turned to sobs, and even Snowball, who jumped up beside her and snuggled close to her body, could not give her any consolation.

13

When Ben reported early the next morning to Miles, the latter's language was unfit for any but the former batman's ears. Boiling in oil and being hung up by the fingernails were mild punishments compared to what he wanted to do to the maid for placing her mistress in such a dangerous predicament.

Ben waited until his master had calmed down somewhat, then said, "Don't be so 'arsh on 'er, sir. She's young and it was easy for a rogue like that to turn 'er 'ead. Besides, even if you fired 'er, I'm sure Lady Arabella would keep 'er on," he said with a lopsided grin.

"I'm caught in a web of my own making, you mean?" Miles suggested. "I suppose you're right, but I'm still going to have her over here and give her a piece of my mind, even if the only time she can get away is in the middle of the night. I'd like to wring her neck."

Ben was still smiling, for he knew Miles Cavendish very well indeed, and if Dora got a light scold, that would be all.

"Aren't you p'raps a bit upset 'cos you're 'avin' to sit 'ere while I 'ave all the fun, milord?" he asked. "Don't forget you'd never 'ave known owt about it if Dora 'adn't brought that letter to me."

For a moment the expression on Miles' face was that of a little boy caught in an act of mischief, then he grinned. "I'm glad you realize, Ben, how frustrating it is to lie here helpless when so much is going on. The worst thing of all is that we now have to wait until he makes another move before we've got a chance of catching him. And having been almost caught twice, he's likely to lay low for a while. I assume that Lady Arabella returned to her bedchamber without anyone knowing she had ever left it?" he said, realizing that it would decidedly complicate matters if Lady Fitzwilliam heard of the escapade.

Ben nodded. "I made sure myself that t'coast was clear afore they went up t'back stairs," he said, "and though t'other servants know Dora's a bit down in t'dumps, they think it's 'cos she's quarreled with 'er gentleman friend."

"Which is, to all intents and purposes, quite true, for she probably told them about having met someone," Miles remarked, then a worried look came into his eyes. "I only wish I knew what Lady Arabella is supposed to have done to warrant such drawn-out threats of bodily harm."

"You don't think, milord, that it might be as well to let 'er know you're trying to 'elp her?" Ben suggested tentatively, but Miles looked quite alarmed.

"Definitely not, for I'm sure she'd be furious with me for putting people in the house to watch her," he said with a rueful grin. "She always had quite a temper when she was aroused, and would, at the very least, refuse to let me render further assistance. Just give a tug on the bellpull, would you, Ben? I'd like to find out if Sir George is up and about as yet, for he must be made aware of this latest incident."

It was a good ten minutes before Sir George Wetherby joined his nephew, for he was in the middle of eating a hearty breakfast. When he was finished, however, he came at once and instructed the butler to follow him with the coffee tray.

Ben looked somewhat embarrassed when the two gentlemen insisted he join them, but they would not take no for an answer even though the dainty coffee cup looked incongruous in his large, work-roughened hands.

When they had finished explaining to Sir George the events

of the previous night, he looked very serious. "He must have known that Arabella has never been in town before, for even a chit just coming out would know that something of that sort was simply not possible," he murmured. "Frankly, I should have thought she would have already acquired a little more town bronze by now. And even if they discussed the wedding, I do not imagine Lady Fitzwilliam even thought to explain just how close those fifty guests would be to Prinny and the family."

"Dora should have known better, though," Miles said testily. "She's been in London most of her life, and should know that Prinny's household staff consider themselves a cut above the staff of other London houses. Even his footmen think they're better than a duke's butler."

There was a pause, then Sir George said, "There's no point blaming the girl, Miles. She seems to think the world of Arabella and would never deliberately harm her. In any case, he'll not try the same thing again. What we need to do now is work out a way of keeping Arabella close to Lady Fitzwilliam at all times, so that the villain cannot accost her when she's alone."

"Without letting Lady Fitzwilliam know about it, of course," Miles added, nodding in agreement. "And perhaps we could find some way of protecting both ladies when they drive about town. Do you have a good rapport with the head coachman, Ben?"

With a wide grin, Ben said, "If that means do I get along with 'im, milord, the answer is yes, but only 'cos I let 'im think 'e's a cut above me. D'you want me to warn 'im?"

Miles pondered the question, then glanced over to Sir George, who nodded firmly. "This is where Dora will have to help, I believe. Perhaps the two of you could let the coachman know that Lady Arabella seems to have an enemy. She could say that she doesn't want to frighten Lady Fitzwilliam by talking to her about it. Then you could suggest he keep a careful watch when they're out. I think that would make most coachmen decide to keep a gun handy in the box beside them.

"I'm afraid I'll have to leave it up to you, Ben, to tell him as little as possible, but enough to make him keep his eyes open, and his mouth closed,'' Miles said, then added with a groan, "If only I'd not been laid up at a time like this.''

"My dear child,'' Lady Fitzwilliam said, a worried expression on her face. "By the looks of you a night's sleep did little good and you should most certainly have slept in this morning. I do hope you're not sickening for something.''

Arabella grimaced as she made her way to a chair by her aunt's side. "I shall be all right in a while,'' she assured her. "I'm still a little tired, but I simply couldn't have stayed in bed a minute longer.'' She turned to thank Dawson for the cup of coffee he had poured for her.

Lady Fitzwilliam grunted. "I know how you feel, for I quickly tire of lying abed myself. Perhaps a little fresh air might be good for you later in the morning. We might go for a drive. Or, better still, would you like to wait until this afternoon and then stop by Miles Cavendish's house to see how he's coming along? Sir George told me last night that he is recovering rapidly but finding a stay in bed most irksome.''

Arabella smiled. "I'm sure he is, for he must have had enough of that when he first suffered the injury. I don't know how he feels about female visitors, but we might as well find out.''

"He'll be happy enough to see you, my dear, I'll be bound. He must love you very much to have forgiven your past behavior. I can think of very few men who would be as kind as he has been to you these last weeks.'' Lady Fitzwilliam reached out a hand and patted Arabella's. "Not that I'm criticizing you for what you did. You were very young and your father should never have had you set out for London unaccompanied.''

Did Miles still love her? Arabella wondered. He had certainly been attentive, but as for love, she didn't know. He hadn't made any attempt to touch her since that one extraordinary kiss, but he had looked at her sometimes in a way that made her heart start to beat quite erratically.

Had he been well and strong, she might easily have spoken to him today about the events of the previous evening. He would have been cross, she knew, at her gullibility, but he was very sensible and would have known what to do. She couldn't tell her papa, for he would have wanted to take her back up north right away.

But she did want to see him very much, and even though there would be no chance for private conversation when accompanied by her aunt, she could at least satisfy herself that he was going along satisfactorily. She would have liked to tell him how much she missed him, but knew that this would be impossible without a degree of privacy and might in any case be encouraging him unfairly.

She helped herself to an egg and a little toast, nibbling almost automatically while her aunt told her about the reception and dinner party she and Sir George had attended the night before; she wished now that she had not been so very stupid and had gone with them instead of believing the lies Dora had so obviously been fed. What a good thing that Ben had followed them and come on the scene when he did!

Arabella suddenly realized that her aunt had asked her a question and she looked at her blankly, murmuring, "I'm sorry, Aunt Gertrude, I didn't hear."

Lady Fitzwilliam frowned severely. "I see you're not quite completely recovered. I wonder if it might be a poor idea to visit Miles, after all. Perhaps you need to have more rest."

"I couldn't bear to spend another minute in bed," Arabella protested, "and I wouldn't miss seeing Miles this afternoon for anything. It was just a momentary lapse, that's all."

Her aunt nodded. "You're probably right, and last evening's entertainments must seem quite dull when related in detail. I do believe that Sir George's company enhances a great many otherwise boring occasions, so I'll not repeat what I was saying. I've no doubt that last night's royal wedding will be the chief topic of conversation at every affair for the next few weeks and will prove much more interesting."

She rose. "I had best attend to yesterday's invitations this morning, for if I do not do so each day, it becomes a quite tedious task. Would half-past-two be a good time for us to start out this afternoon?''

Arabella got up from the table also. ''Of course, Aunt Gertrude, and I do appreciate your suggesting the visit, for I could not, of course, go without you.''

She slipped her hand through her aunt's arm and the two ladies climbed the stairs together, parting at the top to go to their separate chambers. But to Arabella's surprise, when she went into hers, she found the bed still unmade and no sign of Dora even though she rang twice for her. She was, of course, quite capable of tidying the room herself, but her aunt would be quite shocked were she to come in and find her doing so. Instead, she picked up one of the handkerchiefs she was embroidering for her father's birthday and worked on this in the bright light near the window.

Her concentration was somewhat lacking, however, for she found herself stopping occasionally and just staring out into the square, wondering if that awful man was down there somewhere waiting for her to leave the house alone. He would wait a long time if so, for in the small hours of the morning, when sleep was long in coming, she had determined not to venture a foot outside the door again unless her aunt or a trustworthy gentleman was with her.

When Dora did arrive, almost an hour later, her eyes were noticeably reddened, as if she had been crying, but when the maid offered Arabella no explanation, she felt it unkind to pry.

It was unusual for Dora to be silent for long, however, and when Arabella looked up from her work a few minutes later, she saw the girl looking at her hesitantly, then she came over to the window.

''I just wanted to tell you how sorry I am for all the trouble I caused you, milady. If it hadn't been for Ben, I don't know what would have happened to you,'' the distraught maid said, twisting her apron between her hands in her anxiety.

''I should have known better than to believe the story that man told you, my dear,'' Arabella said, smiling faintly. ''For one thing, though you are a most attractive young lady, I doubt that Carlton House footmen associate with any but royal servants.''

Dora nodded. ''And Hanover Square is a long way from Carlton House,'' she added, repeating some of the words that had been said to her not an hour ago. ''If he'd been what he said he was, he'd have been spending an hour or so off in St. James's Square or Green Park, not all this way away.''

Arabella placed her needlework on the table and got up. Putting an arm around the girl's shoulders, she said gently, ''There's no point in blaming yourself for last night, Dora. It's over and done with as far as I'm concerned. I don't know what the scoundrel's motives might have been, but I intend to be a great deal more careful of where I go in the future.''

''Oh, yes, milady, you must,'' Dora said quite fiercely. ''I've lived in London nearly all my life and I've never known anything like this to happen before.''

''Not in this part of London, I'm sure,'' Arabella agreed. ''Now, if you'll help me select a suitable afternoon gown, I'll change and join Lady Fitzwilliam for luncheon. Afterward we intend to pay a call on Lord Cavendish, so I must look my very best.''

She turned toward the armoire and did not notice the look of surprise on Dora's face which was quickly hidden as the two of them searched through the now-considerable number of gowns for the most appropriate one. A gown of blue sarcenet with white embroidery was finally agreed upon, and with it she would wear a matching blue straw bonnet that had white lace under the brim and made Arabella's complexion seem to glow.

''You look a real treat, milady,'' Dora said, feeling almost back to her usual, cheerful self. ''Would you like to take the blue parasol?''

''Not this time,'' Arabella told her, ''for we'll be going out in Lady Fitzwilliam's closed carriage.''

The maid smiled, glad of the information, for this was just the thing to let Ben know about in advance and get her back into his good graces. She held the chamber door open for her mistress to pass through and watched her descend the grand stairs and enter the dining room before hurrying toward the back staircase.

"How lovely you look," Lady Fitzwilliam said as her niece entered the room. "I was just telling Dawson that we will both have a glass of sherry before luncheon. I thought it might bring a bit of color back to your cheeks, but I see you must have rested and achieved the same effect."

Arabella's smile widened. "Don't cancel the order, for it's just what I need to face Miles' possible wrath. You know, I'm sure, that some men hate to have ladies see them when they're at all under the weather."

"Nonsense! Miles is far too good-mannered to let us know, even if he secretly wishes us in Hades. Though I must admit that the marquess heartily disliked having me anywhere near him when he was ill. Come to think of it, though, I didn't fare that much better when he was well," Lady Fitzwilliam added with a dry chuckle.

After a light but delicious luncheon, the two ladies went out to the waiting carriage, and though Arabella was surprised to see Ben sitting next to the coachman, she made no comment.

The Warrington town house was situated on the south side of Grosvenor Square, and Lady Fitzwilliam remembered it well from the days when the former earl and his lady, Miles' parents, used to entertain there quite lavishly.

It was Ben who jumped down and rang the doorbell while the coachman held the horses in check, and a footman helped the ladies alight. A startled butler showed them into the drawing room while he went to inform his master that they had called to see him.

"It's not had a thing done to it, by the look of things, since the countess died," Lady Fitzwilliam pronounced. "That's a painting of her, over the fireplace. Beautiful woman, and as charming as she was lovely."

Arabella couldn't resist walking over to get a closer look at the portrait, and she had to agree with her aunt that she was indeed a good-looking woman. "Miles must have been quite young when he lost her," she said softly. "What a shame!"

"Yes, it was quite a loss to both children. Do you remember his older sister, Jennifer? She married a viscount and went to live somewhere near the Scottish border. I heard they produced quite a brood of youngsters and that must be why she never comes to town."

"I don't really remember her, for she was already married before I was old enough to be of interest to Miles," Arabella said. "He used to mention her quite a lot, but to tell the truth, I'd almost forgotten that he had a sister."

She turned toward the door as the butler came back. "Lord Cavendish will see you now, my ladies," he said. "Follow me."

Arabella allowed her aunt to go ahead of her, for though it had seemed like a good idea when it was first suggested, the closer she came to seeing Miles, the more she felt like turning around and going back.

To her surprise, however, he was sitting up in bed and looking not at all like an invalid.

He held out a hand to her aunt. "Lady Fitzwilliam," he said, "what a pleasure to have you call."

After her aunt was seated, Arabella came forward, and his hand felt strong in hers. There was a warmth tinged with a little amusement in his eyes as he said, "I am delighted to see you, my dear. A most unexpected pleasure. You will stay for tea, of course."

For a minute Arabella had a vision of what must be going on belowstairs at this moment. The kitchen of two bachelors might have a Madeira cake, but it would have little in the way of delicacies, so the cook must be frantically making pastry and dainty biscuits to augment their meager offerings. She turned to her aunt and met that lady's raised eyebrows with an amused nod.

"Of course we will," she murmured to Miles, who seemed to be unaware that he was still holding her hand, "but what we really want to know is how you are feeling, for we understood from your uncle that the operation was an unqualified success."

"The doctor is nothing short of a genius," he told her, making sure to include Lady Fitzwilliam in his glance. "Even though I am not allowed to get up yet for a day or two, I have not felt so comfortable since before I was wounded.

"I was unaware that George had revealed my secret to you. Forgive me for telling you an untruth, Arabella, but I did not wish to cause you undue concern," he said, a look of almost tenderness in his eyes as he thought of all that she had been through last night.

Arabella left her hand in his, for its warmth was giving her more comfort than she would have believed.

"I understand your reasons, Miles," she said, "but I wish you'd felt that we were close-enough friends to tell me the truth yourself."

His fingers squeezed hers and she placed her other hand over his for a moment. He seemed about to say something else, but looked away as Lady Fitzwilliam cleared her throat.

"You should have had it taken care of a long time ago," that lady pronounced, "when you first heard of this brilliant doctor, never mind waiting until my niece came to town before you would leave your lands."

Arabella turned to look at her aunt and in doing so gently withdrew her hand from his. "Miles' trip to London had nothing at all to do with my visit to you and Papa, Aunt Gertrude," she protested. "In fact, he had no idea I was coming here, for I told no one except the Summersons."

Lady Fitzwilliam said nothing, but the look she gave her niece clearly showed her disbelief. She turned to Miles. "I wish we could have brought you news of the wedding, but Arabella was feeling a little out of sorts this morning and we stayed home."

"I'm sorry to hear that. Are you feeling better now?" Miles asked gently, and the color mounted at once in Arabella's cheeks as she murmured a confused affirmative. "That's good. As it happens, I have already heard some stories of the wedding from George, who, in turn, heard them at his club."

Both ladies looked most interested and waited for them a little impatiently.

"Prince William escorted the bride and I understand that she gave her responses distinctly enough to be clearly heard

by every person present, with not a trace of a stammer."
He chuckled. "I'm afraid that the man who told George was
a little less flattering about Princess Charlotte than he might
have been, for he said that she had a heavy, ungraceful tread
as she approached the altar and that her expression was one
of happy triumph."

"Isn't that just like a man, Arabella?" Lady Fitzwilliam
murmured. "Didn't he say what the princess wore?"

Miles grinned. "Nothing very becoming, I'm afraid. Her
gown apparently consisted of layers of silver, with lots of
frills, lace trimmings, and garlands of diamonds, which
served only to emphasize her rather ungainly figure. But at
least she is happy with Prince Leopold and now has a chance
of remaining so for a while."

"And is that all your uncle recalled?" Arabella asked, her
face flushing a little as she thought of the previous evening.

"All I can remember him telling me," Miles said, "but
he'll probably be back before you leave and you'll no doubt
have the opportunity to question him further."

14

Arabella awoke mildly excited, for tonight she would be attending her first London ball. Her Aunt Gertrude seldom accepted invitations to balls, for ladies of her age were rarely asked to dance, and she heartily disliked being made to feel old by having to sit watching the younger ones enjoying themselves.

But the hostess on this occasion, Lady Doncaster, was too good a friend to be able to refuse, so she had accepted and would put a good face on even if she detested every minute of it. Miles was up and about again, and he and Sir George, who was an old friend of Lord Doncaster, had also received and accepted their invitations, so the evening promised to be a somewhat different but most enjoyable affair.

Over the past two weeks Arabella had seen more of Miles than she had expected to in view of his condition. The visit she and Aunt Gertrude made to his home had cleared the way for other informal meetings and had conveniently disposed of any embarrassment he was feeling because of his necessary convalescence.

They had visited again a couple of days later, and she and Miles had played a game of cards while Sir George had shown Lady Fitzwilliam around the town house. It seemed impossible to believe that in only a couple of months, despite her intention to see as little as possible of Miles, they had become, if not yet intimate friends, a little more than close acquaintances.

They laughed and teased each other, but stopped short of that one fatal step that would put them over the edge of friendship and into what . . . courtship? She shook her head, for that would not do. She had never actually been courted, for she had left for London just as her betrothal had been arranged, then married Richard within forty-eight hours of seeing him at the inn.

She knew something that Miles could not possibly know— that she was a very unsatisfactory wife. Richard had told her so over and over again, making it clear that she did not please him in his bed, so that he had been forced to look elsewhere. Also, she was not very good at taking care of herself and making the best of her looks. This had been of the utmost importance when he frequently wished her to distract his opponents. After seeing what a mess her clothes got into and how her hair was never arranged to the best advantage, he had been forced to spend some of his winnings to hire a girl to look after her.

Also, she had not the least idea of how to run a house, for ever since she was a little girl her papa always had a competent housekeeper to make sure everything ran smoothly. And though she had studied the woman and learned much of what needed to be done, once she left home she had no use for such knowledge. She and Richard always stayed at other people's houses for short spells or, when absolutely necessary, in cheap inns or hotels.

Arabella slipped out of bed and over to the armoire, taking out the gown she would wear tonight, and just at that moment Dora came in with her morning chocolate.

The maid sighed, her eyes dreamy. "I never did see anything as beautiful, milady," she said in awe, reaching out a hand to lift the hem of the orchid lace gown, then letting it fall gently back into its folds.

"It's a present from my aunt," Arabella said, sitting on the side of her bed and taking a sip of her chocolate. "She insisted that the deeper mauve embroidery and tiny seed pearls be added on the hem of the skirt and around the neckline and sleeves. It caused a great deal of additional work, but was well worth it for my first ball.''

''Do you really mean it's your very first ball, milady?'' Dora asked in surprise, then flushed as she realized she was being too familiar with her ladyship. ''I'm sorry, I didn't mean that you're too . . .'' she began, but Arabella's laugh stopped her.

''Oh, Dora, please don't apologize. I'm quite old to be attending my first real ball, I know, but I did go to dances given by the local gentry at home, many years ago. However, I'll probably have forgotten all the steps and trip so often over my partners' feet that they'll not ask me again,'' she said with amusement, for she felt sure Miles would not be able to dance again as yet and she did not care what the other young men thought of her.

''They do say you never forget how, milady,'' Dora assured her mistress, then hurried out of the chamber to see where the girl had got to with the warm water.

Arabella hardly noticed the maid leave, for she was trying to recall if she had ever danced with Miles in the old days. She must have, she decided, for he had surely been invited to all the local affairs, but she could not for the life of her remember. She was sure, though, that they had never danced after they were betrothed.

It now seemed to her quite impossible that she could have known Miles as only a friend in those far-off days, and had not even thought of him as anything else until her father had indicated his desire to see her marry this highly eligible neighbor.

She put aside her reminiscences as Dora returned with water to wash in, and it was not until many hours later, when she was back in her bedchamber once more and taking a bath before dressing for the ball, that she had the chance to think of Miles again.

They had danced, for she could now recall how his light gray eyes had darker gray flecks in them when she saw them up close, and how they always seemed to be twinkling quite merrily when he looked at her. His face had been smooth, particularly his brow, but that was before the pain he had suffered from his wound had etched deep lines on his forehead and around his mouth.

Dora placed a towel around her as she stepped out of the bathtub and was patting her dry when a knock sounded on the door and Lady Fitzwilliam came in. She was already dressed, but her hair was not yet arranged, and she chuckled as Arabella stepped from behind the screen.

"Caught you at a bad moment, I see," she said, holding out two jewelry boxes, "but I wanted to bring these to you before Dora does your hair. The larger one is from your papa, and it's the reason I selected that particular gown, and this other one is from me."

Laughingly protesting that this was not her birthday, Arabella reached out a hand and took the larger box. She lifted the lid and tears filled her eyes as she saw the beautiful necklace of pearls and amethysts with long, matching earrings. She sniffed and muttered, "I don't deserve them."

"Nonsense," Aunt Gertrude said briskly. "You've got to forget the past and realize that having you here again has made your father very happy. Now, don't you go crying over these, for that's not the way to accept a gift."

She handed the smaller box to Arabella, who opened it and looked up at her aunt with a grateful smile. "They're exactly what I needed, and if I wasn't holding on to this slightly damp towel, I'd give you a big hug."

"Don't you dare," Lady Fitzwilliam said as she stepped back hurriedly. "I'd best get out of here and let Dora finish getting you dressed. We're having sherry in the drawing room in a half-hour."

When her aunt had gone, Arabella stepped over to the mirror and took out one of the two delicate combs for her hair that were the second gift. It was topped with a lacy design of jewels to match the earrings and necklace, and she now knew why Lady Fitzwilliam had insisted on adding the pearls and embroidery to the gown.

"Come along, Dora," Arabella said. "We'll have to

hurry, for after receiving such gifts I must not show my ingratitude by being late for supper.''

A half-hour later she entered the drawing room and curtsied low. Lord Darnley reached out a hand to help her up, and Arabella was sure that his blue eyes were a little watery.

"You look beautiful, my dear, so very much like your dear mama, and no one would believe you were a day over twenty-one,'' he said huskily.

Arabella touched the necklace. "Thank you so much, Papa,'' she whispered. "I never thought to own anything as lovely.''

"It's high time someone gave you a few fripperies, for it seems that rake you married gave you nothing—or did you have to sell your jewelry?'' her father asked.

Shaking her head, Arabella told him, "There was no money for such things, for it all went on gambling, I'm afraid, so the only jewelry I have, other than my pearls, is made of paste. Although it looks genuine until examined very closely, I know you would not want me to wear that in your company.''

He snorted, then turned to Lady Fitzwilliam. "You did a fine job, Gertrude. I told Dawson to bring champagne tonight instead of sherry, for we've never truly celebrated the return of my little girl.''

"What a good idea, Kenneth, for there's nothing better for putting one in a festive mood,'' Lady Fitzwilliam pronounced, then raised her cheek for Arabella's kiss. "I hope that young man of yours is well enough to attend the ball tonight. I know he accepted, for George told me they had, but I'm not sure if Miles is ready for dancing yet.''

"He'll know what's best for him,'' Arabella said, then added, "but he's not my young man, just a very good friend.''

Lady Fitzwilliam snorted and glared at her niece. "You'll be a fool if you let him get away, young lady, for you'll not meet another like him, I can assure you.''

She turned as Dawson appeared at her elbow with the

drinks on a tray, and then waited, glass in hand, until her brother made a toast.

"To Arabella. May the next few years be happier than the last ones, and may all he dreams come true," he said warmly, then he and his sister raised their glasses and drank.

When Arabella took a sip, the bubbles tickled her nose and she laughed. "How about a toast to Aunt Gertrude, who was responsible for getting us together again?" she suggested, and Lord Darnley happily agreed.

It was a merry threesome that went in to dinner that evening and then proceeded to Lady Doncaster's ball. Miles was already there, with his uncle, and he could hardly take his eyes off Arabella.

"You're going to make every young lady here envious of you," he murmured to her when he at last got her alone for a moment. "You always look lovely, but this evening there's something very special about you."

She laughed softly. "I think it was the champagne that Papa insisted on opening before dinner," she told him. "We were celebrating the return of the lamb to the fold, I believe, perhaps a little belatedly but nonetheless sincerely."

"Your father looks ten years younger than he did a twelvemonth since," Miles remarked. "I still don't know why you found it necessary to stay with Richard's sister for a year."

"At the time I felt I had to, for I couldn't just go to my father and say, 'Here I am.' And it wasn't fair to Aunt Gertrude to expect her to take me in when the duel was the latest *on-dit* in town," Arabella told him. "But I might have done so had I known in advance how utterly miserable I would be with Clarice and her husband."

Miles nodded sympathetically, then saw that it was their turn to go through the receiving line and into the ballroom, where the orchestra could be heard tuning up.

Lady Doncaster welcomed them and introduced her husband and then her youngest daughter, Josephine, for whom the ball was being given. The girl was quite pretty, but looked extremely nervous, and Arabella could not help feeling glad that she had escaped her own come-out ball, though she had paid a high price!

Once in the ballroom, they joined some of her aunt's friends, greeting them as though they had not seen one another for an age, when in fact they had met for tea only a few days before. Lord Doncaster stood waiting with his daughter for the orchestra to start playing, then he led her onto the floor. She was nervous and missed a step twice, then her father whispered something in her ear and she smiled, lifted her head high, and proudly glided around the floor until her brother and her mama, who were also dancing, came over to change partners with her.

"Lord Doncaster must have a very special relationship with his daughter," Miles whispered in Arabella's ear. "He knew exactly what to say to give her confidence in herself."

"Papa and I were always like that before I made such a mess of my life," Arabella said softly, not daring to look at him lest he see the regret in her face.

"I know," he murmured. "That's what it reminded me of, and tonight you look so very much like that girl I was betrothed to so long ago. May I have this waltz, my dear, before all the young men realize what they've been missing so far this Season?"

"Should . . ." Arabella began to ask him, then decided his leg must be strong enough to dance or he'd not have asked her. She took his hand and allowed him to lead her onto the floor.

But he had not gone halfway around the floor before he knew what a big mistake he had made. He was trying not to limp, but the effort was making it twice as painful.

It was so delightful to be in his arms that at first Arabella did not notice what it was costing Miles, then she glanced at his face and saw the grim set of his lips and she realized he was breathing much more heavily than he should be. She deliberately stumbled, then asked, "Could we sit down please, Miles? I think I've hurt my ankle."

At first he believed her, but as she neared the chairs, she limped on the right rather than the left foot, and his look of concern rapidly disappeared.

"Which ankle did you hurt, Arabella?" he asked dryly.
"Or did you manage to damage them both at the same time?"

She bitterly resented his tone, for she had only been trying
to help him, so she pulled herself free of his protecting arm
and hurried to a seat beside her aunt, turning a cold shoulder
to Miles as he seated himself on her other side.

"Why don't you and Sir George get up, Aunt Gertrude?"
she suggested loudly enough for Sir George to hear, "for
there are quite a number of people as old if not older than
you who are dancing right now."

Lady Fitzwilliam turned upon her niece a look of grave
displeasure, but Sir George liked the idea so much that he
leapt up at once and persuaded that mildly protesting lady
to do him the honor. A moment later Arabella realized her
mistake, for now she was left sitting alone with an ominously
silent Miles.

"Isn't it rather soon after the surgery for you to be putting
so much stress on your leg, Miles?" she asked quietly, trying
to make him talk to her.

"Dr. Radcliff did not say so, and he has encouraged me
to give the leg as much exercise as I can," Miles said
abruptly.

He reminded Arabella of a little boy who had to have
everything he could not do spelled out individually, for he
would make a point of doing anything not on the list.

"I really do not believe your doctor expected you to dance
just yet," she murmured, trying not to smile, "and
particularly to do the waltz. I never even thought of your
leg when we got up, or I would have suggested we sit out
the dance."

"I've been an invalid long enough," Miles said gruffly.
Then he asked more gently, "As you won't dance with me,
will you tell me something about Richard? Did he ever say
why he ran off with you? Was it because we were betrothed
and he felt eloping was the only way?"

Arabella looked quickly up at his face, but saw only a
gentleness there and a genuine interest in finding the reason.
"He didn't love me, Miles, if that's what you thought, and

I had never shown the slightest interest in him until he arrived at that first stop on my way to London. I'm afraid he must never have been your true friend, for he was really extremely jealous of you.''

"In what way?" Miles asked softly.

"He resented the way everything came to you so easily. Your father had a much higher rank than his, for his father was only a viscount and that was all Richard could expect to become. Your financial prospects were also very much better. When your father died and you had everything at so young an age, he felt that it was unfair and that you didn't deserve it.'' She looked up into his gentle gray eyes and saw nothing but compassion there.

"I didn't deserve to lose my father so soon, but I doubt that was what Richard meant. You wouldn't recall my father, I'm sure, but he was a hell-or-nothing hunter, always right on the heels of the hounds. He was thrown at a fence one day and broke his neck. With just the two of us left at home, we'd grown very close; I still miss him sometimes.'' He shook his head, unable to understand what had been wrong with Richard, whose own father had been one of the finest of gentlemen. "Did Richard mistreat you, Arabella?" he asked suddenly.

She looked down at her hands, which had tightly clenched in her lap, and deliberately relaxed them. It was a difficult question to answer truthfully. "He didn't beat me, if that's what you're asking," she told him, "except on just a few occasions. But I think he grew to dislike me eventually and wanted me there only to give him the appearance of respectability. Toward the end I saw little of him except while he was gambling, and then I was always close by.''

Miles took a deep breath and let it out slowly so that his voice was steady when he asked, "Do you mean to say that he did not share your bed?"

She kept her head averted. "He did at first, of course, but there were always much more experienced women who were glad to sleep with him, for he was a very good-looking man in his way," she tried to explain. "I never knew where he

slept, and to be truthful, I didn't care, but I had to pretend
that I did or he would have come to me more often just out
of spite.''

"He didn't try to use you at all to help him win, did he?
I mean, ask you to use mirrors or things like that?'' Miles
asked, finally posing the question that he had been leading
up to, for there had to be a reason, sensible or insane, why
someone wished to harm her.

"Of course he did,'' Arabella told him quite matter-of-
factly. "He even said it was my duty as a wife to help him
win. But I'm afraid I was not a very dutiful wife, for I
absolutely refused to help him cheat. It was bad enough that
I had to be there all the time watching him.''

"At his insistence or because there was nowhere else to
go?'' he asked, his eyes narrowing as he began to get a
picture of the life she had lived.

"Most decidedly,'' she said, "whether sick or well I had
to be there.''

"No wonder you looked so remote that day when you stood
there watching the coffin being lowered,'' Miles said,
shaking his head. "If you were not exactly glad, you could
hardly have regretted his death very much.''

"It was quite a relief, as a matter of fact, but I tried hard
not to let Clarice and Sir Brian realize how I felt. I sometimes
wonder how they are going along, for they paid Richard a
considerable sum of money for the use of Barton Grange,
and now it belongs to Richard's heir.'' There was mild
curiosity, but no malice in her voice, for the year she spent
with them did not seem real anymore.

"It must be a tremendous relief to be living now, as you
are, with your aunt and your father,'' Miles said, understanding much more than she realized. "Yet you don't quite
seem as content as you should be under the circumstances.
Is anything else troubling you?''

For a moment Arabella looked startled, wondering if he
had found out about those notes, but there was no way he
could possibly know of them. She had told no one, and
though Dora had seen one of them, it was indeed fortunate
that the girl was unable to read.

As she was about to tell Miles that he was mistaken and she was perfectly happy, she saw her aunt and Sir George returning to their seats. They had no idea she was watching as Sir George carefully seated her aunt, who looked up at him as she gave him her thanks. There was something in Sir George's expression, repeated in her aunt's face, that gave Arabella an unexpected twinge of jealousy. They're falling in love, she thought, and she wondered if they were as yet aware of it. The jealous feeling passed as quickly as it had come, and she felt extremely happy for the two of them. Sir George was one of the nicest men she had ever known, and her aunt was a warm, generous woman who deserved a loving husband after her unhappy marriage to the marquess.

Arabella was unaware that a little smile had started to play around the corners of her mouth until she heard Miles' voice in her ear and felt his warm breath.

"How long has that been going on?" he murmured. "I'd never have guessed."

Arabella's smile had turned into a decided grin as she turned twinkling eyes on his. "Don't say anything to him, whatever you do," she warned, "for they may not realize it yet, either, and I'd hate a wonderful match to be nipped in the bud."

He shrugged. "I don't know about that. George is the finest fellow, but your aunt has always seemed a bit soured on marriage to me."

"Oh, no," Arabella began when she felt a hand on her shoulder and found that her father had joined them.

"I was thinking of spending an hour or so at my club having a game of cards for real money," he said. "I don't think anyone here will even notice an old man's absence, do you?"

"We'll miss you, Papa," Arabella assured him, "but please don't let that stop you, for I'm sure you've more than done your duty by Aunt Gertrude's friend."

As Lord Darnley went over to have a word with his sister, Miles turned to Arabella and asked, "Doesn't it bother you at all when your father plays cards? I should have thought that Richard's gambling would have made you anxious about anyone who plays for higher stakes."

She shook her head. "Papa has always enjoyed a good game of cards and has never bet more than he could afford to lose. I think he's a little old to start changing that habit now, don't you?" she asked. "With Richard, and with quite a few others, gambling is like a disease that's in their blood. I realized after a while that he really couldn't help himself."

Lady Fitzwilliam leaned over to speak to her niece. "Now that my brother has left and you're apparently not dancing," she said, "I would like to suggest that we go into the supper room for a little refreshment and then leave. Even though most people know of Miles' condition, they may start to talk if the two of you sit together here all evening."

Arabella rose with a little more alacrity than Miles would have liked, for he, for one, did not care if people did start talking, but he had no choice but to agree with her aunt's suggestion, and as soon as they had partaken of some of the excellent dishes their hosts had provided, they thanked Lady Doncaster for her hospitality and left.

15

Though it was several weeks since Lady Audrey Cloverdale had met Arabella in the park, she still blamed her for the severe scold her Cousin Miles had delivered that same evening. Had anyone else, including Lord Cloverdale, dared to speak to her in such terms, she would have retaliated instantly in kind, for she had always been so beautiful that she had been wretchedly spoiled by her entire family, with the one exception of Miles.

It was probably because of this that she had always loved him more than anyone else. He had been kind to his little cousin, for it was not in his nature to be anything else, but he had never let her get away with anything since the first time they had met when she was just five years old. On that occasion he had ended by taking her aside, putting her over his knee, and giving her a few hard swats on her bottom.

Needless to say, he had never needed to do so again, but had been the recipient of an adoration that had at times been embarrassing to the extreme. Until her young son, Charles, came along, Miles had always held first place in her heart.

It was therefore not surprising that she had completely forgiven him for the things he had said to her that evening, and had laid the blame instead at Arabella's door. Ever since that night, when she had cried herself to sleep, she had tried to think of ways to get even, without Miles finding out.

She had known Sir William Barton and his wife for a number of years and was pleased when he inherited the title of viscount from a distant cousin, but it was not until they were among her dinner guests one evening that she found, to her delight, that he was related by marriage to Arabella. Now her chance had come.

"I'm so glad you asked us this evening, my dear," Lady Barton said in her usual slightly bored tones, "for when your invitation arrived William had just about decided that we should set out for the north to see how his cousin's poor little widow is getting along. But he put it off again, for we simply could not miss one of your delightful dinners, and now it will be at least a month before we can leave town."

Lady Cloverdale smiled politely. "How kind of you to change your plans on our behalf," she murmured, "but I did not realize you had family in the north."

"Distant family, that is all, but one must do one's duty even so. William inherited property just outside of a small town called Worksop. A town with such a dreadful-sounding name just had to be almost in Yorkshire." Lady Barton shook her head. "I shudder to think what kind of property we will find in a place like that."

Suddenly Lady Cloverdale's eyes opened wide, for Worksop was near Warrington House, and hadn't Uncle George introduced Arabella as Lady Barton? "Did Lord Barton inherit the property quite recently?" she asked, trying not to sound as eager as she felt.

"A little over a year ago, I believe, from a cousin, Richard, whom he'd never even met. Quite frankly, at the time he was reluctant to admit to the relationship because of the scandal." Lady Barton had lowered her voice to a whisper. "I don't know if you recall, but he was the one who was killed last year in a duel, somewhere near the Scottish border I think it was."

Lady Cloverdale had not realized when they met in the park that Arabella was now a widow. She struggled to keep her excitement from showing. "I do recall something of it, but I did not, of course, realize he was a relative of your husband's. If the little widow's name happens to be Arabella, I don't think you need go all that way to meet her." She paused as Lady Barton nodded in surprise. "I saw her in the park only a few weeks ago, driving with her aunt, Lady Fitzwilliam, with whom I believe she is staying."

"Do you mean that the dowager Marchioness of Aylesford is the widow's aunt?" Lady Barton asked, her drooping eyelids lifting, for once, in amazement. "And there William has been letting her remain in her husband's old home because he understood she had nowhere else to go. Just wait until I tell him."

Fortunately for Lady Cloverdale, dinner was just about to be served, and as she had seated the husband and wife some distance apart, they did not have the opportunity to talk about the little widow until they were on their way home. Of course, she did not at all mind Arabella becoming the latest *on-dit,* but she did not want Miles to ever find out that it had all started at one of her dinner parties. After all, what had she done except tell the truth: that Arabella was not staying in the north but was living in town with her aunt?

Although Lady Barton was considerably older than herself, Lady Cloverdale had quite correctly assessed the lady's penchant for gossip, but what she had not taken into consideration was the influence Viscount Barton had upon his wife.

The next morning, at a reasonable hour, he set out to visit his late cousin's wife, and though he was accompanied by Lady Barton, he had made it quite clear to her that the only reason for taking her along was in case the aunt might be out and the little widow reluctant to receive a gentleman alone.

Lady Barton was not to take any part in his questioning of the young lady, nor was she to repeat any of the information he received to any of her friends without his permission.

When the carriage drew up outside the house in Hanover Square, the two of them alighted and walked up the steps of a house very much grander than the one they occupied in town. A few minutes later, they were shown into the elegant drawing room and told by Dawson that Lady Arabella and Lady Fitzwilliam would join them shortly.

"It's Richard's heir and his wife," Arabella told her aunt, who had readily agreed to see them with her. "And though I've never been in touch with him, I'm almost sure that Clarice and her husband have communicated with him in my name."

"How disgusting," Lady Fitzwilliam observed. "I'm not sure that I want you to have anything to do with members of that family again."

"I saw Lord Barton's first letter, Aunt Gertrude, and it was very kind and helpful. If he wrote further, however, the letters must have been taken out of the post by Clarice."

They had now come within hearing of the drawing room, so they remained silent until they stepped inside.

Viscount Barton came forward and introduced himself first to Lady Fitzwilliam and then to Arabella, beckoning his wife over to meet them.

Lady Fitzwilliam gave instructions to Dawson that refreshments were to be served, then took her place on a couch beside her niece.

"Now, Lord Barton," she began, once they were all seated, "my niece tells me that you very kindly wrote her giving permission for her to remain at Barton Grange while she was in mourning for her late husband."

"I did indeed, my lady, for I had no idea that she had any family either in the neighborhood or here in London," the viscount said quietly. "And her reply thanked me and confirmed her homeless state." His voice held a hint of reproach.

Arabella cleared her throat and glanced at her aunt, who inclined her head. "I did see that letter, my lord, and I was very grateful for your kind offer. At the time I was estranged from my father, and as he was staying here with his sister, it did actually leave me with nowhere to go. But it was not I who replied to that or any other letters you wrote."

The viscount's eyebrows rose perceptibly. "I wrote three letters in all to you and received a total of three replies. Do you mean to tell me that you did not write those responses? And if it wasn't you, then who had the audacity to write to me and append your name?''

There was nothing to do but tell him the truth, Arabella decided, for he appeared to be a reasonable, responsible gentleman.

"Either my sister-in-law or her husband wrote any replies that were sent to you, but before you condemn them out of hand," she warned, "I think you should be made aware of their reasons for doing so. Richard asked for and received from them a considerable sum of money. In return, they were to have the use of the house for the rest of their lives or, of course, until his death. Naturally, neither party expected his demise to be so imminent. I believe that in view of their expectations, they felt justified in trying to remain there as long as you would allow it.''

"That's Cousin Clarice, isn't it, and she married a younger son, a Brian Summerson?" Lord Barton asked.

Arabella nodded.

"I assume it is not your intention to go back there?" he said. When she gave a slight grimace and a shake of her head, he asked, "What condition is the place in? Is it in need of repairs and is there much land that goes with it?''

He's kind but he is a businessman, Arabella thought. "The house could use some work, but all the necessary things are taken care of. I'm afraid, however, that there was virtually no land in the entail, so Richard sold all the original lands piece by piece as he needed more money.''

"For gambling, I assume?" the viscount offered dryly, and Arabella nodded.

"It is a family flaw—occurs about once in each generation or two," he stated flatly. "Fortunately, I was spared.''

There was a knock on the door and Dawson came in with a tray of tea and savories. He placed it close to Lady Fitzwilliam, and she poured while Lord Barton silently debated what he should do.

Arabella rose and handed around the dainty cups, then passed the savories.

Lord Barton absently reached for one and finished it before

taking a sip of tea, then he set the cup firmly in its saucer.

He looked across at Arabella. "I'm glad you were frank with me about the extenuating circumstances, for my first inclination was to turf them out on their ears," he said gruffly, "and it was kind of you, for though you did not say so, I get the feeling that you have little love for the pair of them."

Arabella smiled faintly while her aunt gave a decided snort.

"I see no reason why the Summersons should get completely away with their little scheme, but on the other hand, I believe that they paid highly for only a short residence there. Like your husband, they took a gamble and lost," he said. "What would you think of my allowing them to stay there indefinitely providing they keep up the property? Of course, I would go and inspect the place before making the offer, and pay them a visit once a year, but never at quite the same time, so they couldn't be sure of when I might come."

"I think you're being very kind, but you might change your mind once you meet them, so don't go with too definite a plan," Arabella warned, a smile hovering around the corners of her mouth.

"How did you know that my niece was in London and where you might find her?" Lady Fitzwilliam asked curiously. "Although I know the name, I don't recall having met you in town this Season."

"It was purely by chance," Lord Barton remarked. "Lady Barton and I were thinking of leaving to take a look at the place when we got a dinner invitation we did not like to refuse. My wife was explaining this to our hostess and it seems that she had seen you in the park quite recently, but did not know we were related. She knows Lady Arabella best under her maiden name, I believe."

"Was it Lady Cloverdale?" It was Lady Fitzwilliam who posed the question.

"Yes, as a matter of fact. She and her husband have been good friends of ours for a number of years despite the difference in our ages," Lord Barton told her.

With the matter settled to all intents and purposes, the couple left soon after finishing their refreshments.

Once they were out of the house, Lady Fitzwilliam turned to her niece. "You handled that extremely well, my dear. I was proud of you. But what a pity it is that Miles' beautiful cousin now knows about Richard. I don't think Lord Barton would have told me if I had not asked the question directly."

"Well, at least we'll know from where they come if a few nasty little insinuations start to be made," Arabella said a little sadly, for she had recently found herself enjoying the Season very much and would be sorry if she had to suddenly leave town.

When she returned to her bedchamber, however, there was yet another reason for regret. On her dressing table there was a letter addressed to her—an exact replica of the other anonymous notes.

"Are you sure this is an exact copy?" Ben asked Dora when she gave him a paper on which she had printed the words of this latest note, for delivery to their master.

"Of course it is," the maid snapped.

"NOT MUCH LONGER TO WAIT NOW. I'M ACROSS THE STREET, AROUND THE NEXT CORNER, BEHIND YOU, SO CLOSE I COULD TOUCH YOU—AND I WILL."

" 'Is lordship isn't goin' to like this one bit, I can tell you," Ben muttered as he made ready to leave with it. " 'Ow did 'er ladyship seem to take it?"

"She's scared out of her wits, and I should think so, the poor love. Just imagine him sending notes like that to such a kind young lady," Dora said. "He wasn't a bit like that when I first met him."

"You'd best be ready to come an' see 'is lordship an' tell 'im again just what that feller you met looked like," Ben warned, "for 'e'll need to know as much as 'e can about 'im."

It was only fifteen minutes later that Ben handed the note to Miles and saw his master in one of his rare rages.

"When I finally get my hands on him, he'll rue the day

he started this persecution," he roared. "Arabella must be quite terrified and almost too frightened to go out of the house at all. Did she say anything to Dora?"

Ben shook his head. "The girl knew what it was, 'cos it was still there on t' bed, but Lady Arabella thinks she can't read. She told me that 'er ladyship was lyin' down, as white as t'bedsheets, an' said she couldn't eat a bite of lunch."

"Who can we get to help you, Ben," Miles asked, "for I want a constant guard on her from now on. Is your brother, Ted, in town?"

"Aye, 'e is, and right glad 'e'd be to 'elp," Ben told him.

"Good, get him over there right away and then the two of you can take turns to see that she's never outdoors alone. The man must have been very sure of himself when he let Dora see him, but you can guarantee that her description won't help now, for he's going to be wearing a disguise in the future. He must be quite mad, which makes him even more dangerous." Miles sighed in frustration. "If only she would talk about it, even to her aunt, it would be so much easier. Having to guard her without her knowledge makes it twice as difficult, for she could do the wrong thing without meaning to."

Ben shook his head. "Couldn't you let 'er know some'ow that you know wot's goin' on?"

"No, Ben, I know her too well for that. She'd be furious that I'd spied on her, and she might not let me do anything at all to help. Sir George will assist me in keeping an eye on her at the various entertainments we go to, of course, while you or Ted watch the outside. My uncle seems to be on much closer terms than before with Lady Fitzwilliam, and I think I'll leave it up to him as to whether to tell that lady or not," he mused. "At least, if she knew, she could make up reasons for riding back and forth in one carriage instead of using two separate ones."

"It's a mystery again 'ow the letter got 'ere, milord," Ben said grimly. " 'E 'as to know someone at the 'ouse, for Mr. Dawson 'as claimed each time that it appeared from nowhere. One minute the 'all table was bare, and t'next there was the letter on it."

"And this last one was delivered so mysteriously also?" Miles asked grimly.

Ben nodded. "It seems that way. It just appeared on't'all table and Dawson sent it upstairs with one of t'maids."

Miles looked suddenly alarmed. "Is the door, by any chance, left unlocked and unattended during the day, then?"

"It's not supposed to be," Ben declared. "If Dawson's not around, there's supposed to be a footman on duty in t' 'all. Per'aps 'e's being paid to look t'other way and then say nowt."

"Perhaps you're right," Miles said softly. "Do you think there is any way you could start questioning the footmen without their becoming suspicious?" He saw Ben shaking his head and said ruefully, "No, I suppose you're right. A groom doesn't rank high enough for that. Maybe we should have Dora befriend one of the footmen and start asking a few questions."

Ben smiled. "That's the way, sir," he said. "She's a bonny lass an' might just find summat out."

Thanking Ben for his prompt action in bringing the note, Miles sent him back to Hanover Square, but not before having him write a note to his brother, Ted, telling him Lord Cavendish needed him right away. This was to be delivered by one of Miles' servants who would bring Ted back at once, if that was at all possible.

The next thing was for Miles to discuss the whole affair with Sir George when he returned from taking Lady Fitzwilliam for a drive.

"Is she still not feeling well?" Lady Fitzwilliam asked Dawson when she returned from her drive in the park and found that Arabella was still lying down.

The old butler looked around to be sure no one was within earshot, then asked, "Might I have a word with you in private, my lady? There's something very strange going on of which I think you should be made aware."

"Of course, Dawson," she said, quite ready to listen to a servant who had been with her so long. "Come into the library, where the door is so thick that no one will hear a word.''

When the door was closed behind them and Lady Fitzwilliam had seated herself behind the large oak desk that had been in her late husband's family for generations, she said, "Now, Dawson, tell me what is worrying you so.''

"It's Lady Arabella, milady,'' he began. "Letters keep arriving for her by the strangest of ways. Not a single footman will admit to receiving them; they just appear on the hall table as if a ghost had placed them there.''

Lady Fitzwilliam looked a trifle disbelieving. "Come, now, Dawson,'' she protested, "you know better than that. Lady Arabella probably has a secret admirer and he has paid one of the servants to put them there when no one is around. How long has this been going on?''

"Almost since she arrived, milady,'' he told her, then looked thoughtful for a moment. "I remember now when the first one came. It was there the morning after the party you gave for her ladyship. It wasn't there when I checked the house before retiring, but it was on the hall table the next morning before I drew the bolts on the front door.''

"Then someone must have brought it to the back door,'' Lady Fitzwilliam said firmly.

But Dawson shook his head. "Cook assured me that she unlocked the back door herself that morning, milady. Later in the day, I questioned the entire staff and they all swore they'd never set eyes on it before.''

"Has anyone new been hired this Season? Someone you don't know and trust, perhaps, as much as the old staff?'' his mistress suggested.

"That's just it, milady. You see, there's Dora, and though we all like her and I'd swear she worships her mistress, she has been seen slipping out sometimes when she thought no one noticed.'' He looked grim. "But she's the one who started asking questions about how the letters got here, and she'd hardly do that if she was the culprit, now, would she?''

"She might if she was unusually clever,'' Lady Fitzwilliam suggested. "Has she ever said why she was asking?''

Dawson put a hand on the desk and, leaning forward, said

in a lowered voice, "She said the letters frighten Lady Arabella, and it must be true, for the last one seems to have put her in her bed."

Lady Fitzwilliam sat for a while, absently fingering one of the ledgers on the desk as she debated what to do, for it was a more serious matter than she had at first thought.

Finally she looked up at Dawson and smiled a little wearily. "I think I'll have a word with my niece, not tell her of our conversation, of course, but see if there is anything she would like to talk to me about. Please don't say anything of this to anyone else, Dawson, particularly my brother, for I don't want him needlessly worried if it should turn out to be nothing."

16

In the early hours of the morning, when sleep was proving to be quite elusive, Arabella decided that she was not going to let herself become a scared ninnyhammer, afraid of her own shadow. She would go out and do all the things that she had been enjoying, but just be sure that someone was with her at all times. They did not have to know she was in danger, but their very presence should keep the man away.

Having reached this decision, she lay for a while thinking of Miles and how very much he had come to mean to her in the short time she had been in town. Then, after a while, her eyes closed and she slept.

Several hours later she rose, but could not completely carry out her plan, for Dora had brought her a light breakfast and so she did not go downstairs to eat as she had intended.

Her toilet was more lengthy than usual, for she was determined to remove all traces of sleeplessness from her face, and then she changed her mind about the gown she would wear, selecting a new one in deep-gold muslin trimmed with white satin ribbons at the high waist, which did not make her look quite so pale. The long sleeve beneath the short puff one would make it quite suitable if her aunt decided they would go out this morning. Dora took out the matching bonnet and hurried off to iron the ribbons while Arabella went downstairs to the library, where Lady Fitzwilliam could usually be found at this time of day.

She opened the door and strode in without pausing to knock, expecting her aunt to be pouring over ledgers, and was quite flustered when she found that Miles was with her and they were in seemingly earnest conversation.

He rose immediately and took Arabella's hand. "How are you today, my dear?" he asked gently. "I was so sorry that you were feeling a bit down pin yesterday."

"It was nothing, really, just a little megrim, that's all," she said, not needing to force a bright smile, for she was very happy to see him. Just his being there gave her confidence, a feeling that nothing bad could happen when he was looking at her the way he was at this moment.

"I was just inquiring about you," he told her truthfully, intentionally not adding what the exact topic of their conversation had really been. "Do you feel well enough to take a drive in the park with me?"

Despite her previous determination, the thought of leaving the safety of the house and going out where her tormentor might be lurking frightened her for a moment. Miles felt a slight jerk as her fingers tightened in his and he could not help but squeeze them reassuringly.

"That would be lovely," Arabella said, then turned to ask, "Will you be joining us, Aunt Gertrude?"

"Not this morning, for I've been shirking my duties here of late," her aunt said, pointing to the ledgers. "Why don't you run upstairs and get your bonnet? The fresh air will do you good."

When her niece had left, Lady Fitzwilliam's smile disappeared and she looked anxiously at Miles. "You will take good care of her, won't you?"

"Of course I will," Miles assured her. "One of my two men who are posted here will be with us, and as I told you earlier, I will guard her with my life."

"I'm so glad we had this talk today, Miles," she said

gratefully, "for after speaking to George last night, I was quite sick with worry. Now that I know you are taking every precaution I feel a great deal better, but I won't be sure that she's completely safe until the man's in jail, where he belongs."

They went into the hall then to wait for Arabella, and a few minutes later she came hurrying down the stairs and placed her hand in Miles'.

"You're sure you won't change your mind?" Arabella asked her aunt, who shook her head and smiled.

"Just enjoy yourselves," she said, "and perhaps you'll join us for luncheon, Miles, when you return?"

"It will be my pleasure, my lady," he told her, then slipped Arabella's hand through his arm and went out to where his phaeton waited, with Ben at the horses' heads.

Though the leg was not yet completely healed and would not be for some time, Miles was walking now with a limp so slight that it was scarcely discernible. He helped Arabella into the carriage, then went to the other side and climbed in, taking the reins from Ben's hands.

He deliberately made small talk until the stiffness in Arabella's shoulders relaxed. In one more attempt to persuade her to tell him her fears, he said, "You seem rather tense today, my dear. Is there anything I can do to help?"

She turned her head quickly toward him, startled, then said sharply, "I'm not tense at all, really, just enjoying the fresh air on my face, that's all. And your company, of course."

"That's good," he said gently, hoping she meant it. "Have you heard anything from your sister-in-law since you left the north?"

Arabella laughed. "No, and I hope not to hear anything either, but I'm afraid there's a chance that I may. You see, I had a visit from Richard's heir, Viscount Barton."

Miles reined in the horses to wait until they could cross Park Lane and enter the park, then he gave his full attention to Arabella. "I know the fellow, but was not aware that he and Richard were related, for they're not at all alike. Did he just wish to make your acquaintance?"

"It was a little more than that," Arabella said with a short laugh, "for Clarice and Brian have been corresponding with him in my name, so he thought I was still living at Barton Grange until your Cousin Audrey told him I was in town."

Miles' eyes narrowed and he said nothing for a moment, then asked, "Do you think Audrey was trying to make trouble for you?"

"Not in just telling them I was in town, and Lord Barton seemed a very sensible sort of man. I doubt that they talk very much of their connection with Richard in view of the scandal involved," she said matter-of-factly.

"His wife is one of the biggest gossips in town," Miles said bitterly, "so the damage may already have been done."

Arabella put a hand on Miles' knee. "Don't worry about it, Miles. I've had a lovely time here with you, Aunt Gertrude, and Sir George. If the scandal should start up again, I really won't mind going back to Darnley Hall with Papa, for I will have something good to look back upon."

They were in the park now, and Miles drew the phaeton over to where some trees gave them a modicum of privacy. It would be obvious to anyone looking that way that a carriage was there, but its passengers would be completely hidden by the spring foliage. He would have liked to have stepped down and taken her for a walk alone, but knew that it was too dangerous at the moment.

Instead, he tried the reins, checked to be sure that Ben was keeping a sharp lookout, then turned toward her. Taking both of her hands in his and gazing into her beautiful eyes, he asked, "Will you marry me, Arabella? I promise I will cherish you and protect you and do my utmost to make you happy."

He knew she was going to refuse when the tears filled her eyes, but he was quite prepared to wait and press his suit until she did agree.

"I can't, Miles," she whispered brokenly. "You're far too good for me, for I'm no longer the innocent young girl you were betrothed to before."

"You're not," Miles agreed softly. "You're a much better

person than that spoiled little brat who just had to have a Season in London before being officially betrothed. Marry me, my love, for I know you'll make me the happiest of men, and I'll try my very best to do the same for you."

"You don't know everything about me, Miles," she said quietly, placing her fingers against his lips to stop the protest he was about to make, "and I'm very glad that you don't, for I'd hate to see you disillusioned. I had no right to come here and place a burden on my aunt and Papa. Don't blame Audrey, for she had little to do with it, but I've also decided to ask Papa if I may go home, alone, and stay at Darnley Hall. Please try to understand," she begged.

Though she didn't tell him so, she meant to face her tormentor alone and not place others in danger by trying to protect her. Perhaps because he loved her so much, Miles read it clearly on her face; he drew her into his arms, pressing her cheek against his. He felt as though he had always loved her, but never so much as at this moment.

"Don't do anything for a few days, my love, for sudden decisions are not always the right ones. If you're of the same mind in, say, a week from now, I'll help you with your plans for leaving, I promise," he said softly.

She felt his warm breath on her ear and unconsciously moved even closer as she thought about what he had said, "I'll wait a week, for you're right about quick decisions, but I couldn't allow you to go to any further trouble on my behalf."

The soft brush of her lips against his cheek was too much for Miles, and he turned his head so that his own lips lightly touched hers. He felt her gasp and she murmured, "You mustn't, Miles, you really mustn't," while making not the slightest move to withdraw her face from his.

His hand slipped behind her head as his lips applied a gentle but firm pressure, and suddenly there was no need for even the gentle force. She was eagerly kissing him in return, letting his tongue play games with hers and murmuring deep in her throat with the pure pleasure of it.

He could feel the rapid beat of her heart through her thin

gown as he pressed her nearer to him and then her arms were around his neck, drawing him closer and closer until they seemed molded together. They might have stayed there all morning, oblivious of carriages passing a little distance from them, their arms entwined, lost to everything except their own intense feelings, but Miles suddenly realized something was wrong.

There was the sound of coughing, as though someone was about to choke, and Miles realized it was Ben who must have been trying to attract his attention for some time. With the utmost regret he gently raised his head and gazed for a moment at Arabella's flushed cheeks and slightly glazed blue eyes with just a hint of a question in them.

Then he looked across to where Ben was standing, making so much noise that an interested observer might have thought him choking to death. Few members of the *ton* were, however, at all interested in the actions of a lowly tiger, and carriages were passing a short distance from him without anyone taking the slightest notice.

"What is it, Ben?" Miles called softly.

Ben continued to cough and sputter at intervals, while motioning to where a man, mounted on a fine black gelding, sat under another clump of trees some distance away. He appeared to be looking at the passersby, but every ten seconds or so his glance would return to the phaeton.

Without turning his head completely in that direction, Miles watched the man, then suddenly his attention was drawn back to his own carriage, for Arabella had somehow managed to jump down and had gone over to see what she could do to help the tiger. She had a hold of Ben's arm and was saying, "Now, just try to take deep breaths and then let them out slowly, and you'll soon be all right."

Though Miles wanted to laugh, he would not have done so and hurt Arabella for anything in the world. What a dear girl, he thought, to go to the fellow's aid like that. He'd better tell Ben to find a method of signaling, in the future, that was less startling to a young lady of such tender sensibilities.

He glanced across to where the rider had been observing

them, but there was now no one at all under those trees, and a quick glance around revealed not a single rider answering the watcher's description. He tried to get a picture in his mind of what the man had looked like, but it was no good. He had not seen him clearly enough and could only recall that he was slim and sat straight in the saddle, a description that might fit any fellow up to the age of thirty or so, after which men tended to thicken.

Ben was thanking Arabella as he helped her up into the phaeton, then he jumped on the back as Miles eased the horses forward into a gentle trot and slipped into the stream of park traffic.

"Are you and your aunt going to the Everslys' card party this evening?" Miles asked. "I know the play will be too tame for your father, but George and I thought we might go, for, as you know, we neither of us play for high stakes as a rule."

"Yes, my aunt did mention it yesterday, as I recall. They're particularly close friends of hers and she wouldn't think of declining except for the very best of reasons," she told him, then chuckled as she admonished, "She also said that they're inclined to serve a quite extravagant supper, so don't stuff yourselves before you go there."

He laughed. "Thanks for the warning. I see you must have noticed that my girth has increased somewhat since coming to London. It's a good thing the Season doesn't last all year, for the way these hostesses try to outdo one another we'd scarcely be able to walk around."

Arabella made a pretense of looking him up and down critically, then realized how very much she liked what she saw, and did it again, a little more discreetly this time. He had always cut a fine figure, for, despite his remarks, he was very active and did not overeat. His face was a little more lined than it had been six years ago, but there was still no question that he was one of the handsomest men in town this Season.

"Do I pass muster, ma'am?" he asked with an impish grin.

"I believe I see a fleck of dust on your boots, sir, and it's rather fortunate for you that Brummell has now left England, for your cravat would never have passed his sharp eye,'' she drawled affectedly, ''and your hair is just a trifle too long for a perfect *à la Titus.*''

Though he still grinned, the way he automatically reached up to give a tug at his cravat and ran a hand around the back of his neck caused Arabella to laugh out loud.

''Now, see here, young lady, I didn't bring you into the park to be laughed at,'' he told her, wagging a finger in her direction though his smiling face showed how pleased he was that she could still tease.

''You didn't let me finish,'' Arabella protested wickedly, ''and now I may never tell you the rest.''

''My lady,'' he said gravely, though his eyes refused to comply, ''I tender my profound apologies and beg you with all my heart to please continue. Were it not for the scarcity of room I would go down on my knees and plead with you to do so.''

''Please don't try,'' she told him, trying hard to suppress her laughter. ''All I was going to say was that, despite those small imperfections, you are without doubt . . . .'' She paused, then ended quite seriously, ''You are without doubt the most handsome gentleman in this park today and I am very proud to be in your company.''

He knew it was just a sop for having refused his proposal of marriage, but he was glad that she had wanted to offer one, and he reached over for her hand and squeezed it gently.

When they returned, Lady Fitzwilliam was pleased to see a little color in Arabella's cheeks, but when her niece ran upstairs to take off her bonnet, Miles' careful survey of the street from each and every window considerably alarmed the older lady.

''Do you really believe that he is watching the house so closely?'' she asked him when he returned to the drawing room.

''I'm very much afraid he may be,'' Miles replied. ''I don't think she should go with you to pay calls this afternoon.''

Dawson had left a tray with four glasses of sherry on the

sideboard, and as Miles spoke, he picked up one and brought it to where she sat, placing it on the small table at her side. As he turned to go back for his own, she touched his sleeve lightly and he looked down at her worried face.

"Perhaps if you stayed in also she would not take exception to it?" he suggested, hoping she would agree, then added, "You are going to the Everslys' tonight, I believe. Why don't George and I pick the two of you up here at whatever time is most convenient for you?"

Lady Fitzwilliam looked somewhat relieved at his suggestion. "That will take care of today, but what about tomorrow and the next day? She's not foolish, and if it goes on for long, she is bound to realize that we know about the letters."

"Please stop worrying and permit me to do it for you," he begged. "I have the strangest feeling that he is coming to the end of his patience and that the next few days will see it through."

There was the sound of Arabella's light footsteps outside. She came hurrying in, picking up her glass of sherry from the tray as she passed. "You two look like a couple of conspirators," she said jokingly. "Have you been talking about me while I've been gone?"

Lady Fitzwilliam laughed lightly. "But, of course, my dear. What else could we possibly have been talking about?"

Miles smiled as he courteously stepped forward and placed her sherry on a nearby table, then held a chair for her to sit down.

"Thank you, Miles," she murmured, thinking to herself how perfectly unnecessary but at the same time very nice it was to have a gentleman assist one in this way. Her brother-in-law seldom thought of helping his wife, let alone an unwanted guest, and as for Richard, such courtesies were displayed only in public to impress his gambling acquaintances.

She gave a start when the doorbell sounded, but was relieved when Sir George Wetherby was shown in.

"Oh, dear," Lady Fitzwilliam exclaimed, "I completely

forgot to tell you that I sent a note to Sir George after you left, asking him to join us for luncheon. My memory is really not quite what it used to be.''

The two gentlemen left a couple of hours later, after arranging to call for them that evening. Sir George had taken a hackney to Hanover Square, so they left in Miles' phaeton and had not gone very far before the conversation came around to Arabella.

''We've been so busy, these last few days, in trying to protect her that I've completely forgotten to ask you how your campaign is coming along,'' Sir George remarked. ''I thought that when the young lady insisted on visiting you while you were confined to your bed, things would soon come to a head, but it would now appear that I was mistaken.''

''I cannot claim great success as yet, I'm afraid,'' Miles said a little morosely, ''but I still have high hopes. Just this morning, while we were in the park, I tried my best to persuade her to tell me what was troubling her, but I'm afraid my efforts were in vain. She's even considering going home to Darnley Hall alone should the old scandal raise its ugly head again.''

''Is there any reason to think it might?'' Sir George asked, frowning.

Miles nodded. ''After I drop you, I'm going to take a run over to the Cloverdales' place. Audrey has found out about the duel, and I want to reinforce my previous threats.''

''Don't drop me anywhere. I'll go along with you and make sure she realizes we're serious,'' Sir George said. ''Arabella has enough problems without Audrey giving her a few more.''

''I've never believed in turning down reinforcements, George. By all means come with me if you have the time,'' Miles agreed, ''but to change the subject somewhat, aren't you, also, paying rather a lot of attention to a certain lady?''

''We're not all slow tops, you know,'' Sir George growled. ''I always admired Gertrude's pluck in standing up to that crass fellow her family made her marry. Now I find that there's a good deal more to her than courage. She's a warm, understanding woman and I am considering breaking a vow of many years' standing and launching a campaign of my own.''

''Well, George, I wish you more success than I'm having, but perhaps we'll both come out all right in the end.'' Miles slowed to go through the Hyde Park turnpike, then continued along the Knightsbridge Road toward his young cousin's house.

17

In the early evening crush of carriages, the Everslys' house was at least a half-hour ride from Hanover Square, though one athletically inclined might have walked it with minutes to spare. Situated on Curzon Street, a rather busy thoroughfare near Shepherd's Market, it was large in size compared to its neighbors and only a few houses away from the Mayfair Chapel. Unlike most others in the area, which had small gardens in the back, the houses on this portion of Curzon Street backed onto the Bear and Ragged Staff Mews, where the guests' carriages and coachmen would await their masters' departure.

At the appointed hour, Lady Fitzwilliam and Arabella, accompanied by Miles and Sir George, alighted at the front door and were immediately greeted by their hostess. She and Lady Fitzwilliam had been bosom bows at their come-outs many years ago, and had remained friends ever since, so they had much to talk about but could not delay the other guests waiting to be received, so they agreed to meet at the same table for supper.

Champagne was being served in the drawing room, where earlier arrivals waited to be assigned tables in the several rooms set up for card play, and Lady Fitzwilliam went over to greet someone she had not seen for several days. A few minutes later, Sir George joined her.

Miles had noticed that Arabella had become quite nervous again. She kept looking around the room and occasionally glanced behind her as elegantly dressed people wandered in and out. One thing was certain: Miles had no intention of letting her out of his sight tonight, for he had the instinctive feeling, probably emanating from his service in the army, that the enemy was close by.

While Miles waited with Arabella, Tom Coachman waited also as he slowly took the Cavendish carriage around to the mews in the back, for there was already quite a crush here and a long line of carriages ahead of him. He'd been surprised that a second coachman plus Ben and his brother, Ted, were on duty tonight, for usually no more than two of them went with the carriage in town, but he was happy enough, for now they could have a hand or two of cards on their own.

When he suggested to Ben that he send the other coachman to the White Horse for a bottle of gin, Ben made no objection, for it would be a long night and one bottle would not go far enough between the four of them to cause any mistake in judgment. Ben had already taken a good look around but had not seen anyone resembling the fellow who had accosted Lady Arabella that other time, but he still intended to keep a sharp lookout. It seemed his lordship had a hunch about tonight, and his hunches had paid off many a time when they were out in Spain.

" 'Ave you seen anyone like the feller we're lookin' for?" Ted had come over and joined Ben, who was perched on the back of the coach.

Ben shook his head. " 'E could be any of 'em, for all I know. If 'e is 'ere, 'e's not goin' to look like 'e did afore. T'master thought it was 'im we saw this mornin' in t'park, but 'e was too far away to tell."

In the night air, Ben's voice carried farther than he had intended. Deep in the shadows of another coach, where no one could see, a satisfied smile came over the face of what looked like a decrepit old drunk who crouched low, shoulders hunched, an empty gin bottle in his hand, and an expectant gleam in his eyes. He'd known at once that he had the right carriage, for the Warrington family crest was emblazoned on the sides, and now he knew also that they were expecting him, which just added to the excitement and sharpened his thirst for revenge.

Presently the coachman came back with the gin, and the four of them settled down to a quiet game of whist, a pleasant-enough way to pass the time until the carriage was needed once more.

Meanwhile, inside the house the card party was in full swing. Lady Eversly knew it was a success when she realized that though they had put out a great many more card tables than she thought they would need, there were not enough and she had to send servants hurrying upstairs to the attic to bring more down.

She smiled happily at her friend, Lady Fitzwilliam, who gently chided her, "And there you were so sure that no one would want to attend a simple card party after all the balls and dinners held to celebrate the royal wedding."

"You know how it is, Gertrude," Lady Eversly said with a sigh. "Many people send out acceptances to every invitation they receive and then attend whichever ones they're in the mood for when the evening comes around. I always go in fear and trembling that someone much more interesting than I will be entertaining on the same night."

"Isabel, you should do what I do and then you'd have nothing to worry about," Lady Fitzwilliam advised. "I've now reached the stage where I only invite my closest friends, as I did for the party I gave when my niece arrived, and then I know for sure that they'll all come even if they're at death's door."

"They'll all come because they do not want to offend a most influential and charming marchioness." Lady Casterfield, who had come out the same year as the other two ladies, smiled at Sir George when he drew up a chair for her. "And then, of course, with Byron and Brummell no longer in the country, everyone is looking for someone with wit to replace them.''

"That young man overstepped himself,'' Lady Eversly pronounced. "I do declare it has come to a sorry pass when the son of a servant feels he can insult the heir to the throne and get off scot-free.''

"Now, Isabel,'' Lady Casterfield said gently, "a private secretary is not quite a servant, you know, and the quarrel was some years ago.''

"I know it was, and if the Prince had been more popular, that young man would have been completely ostracized long since,'' Lady Eversly affirmed. "I'm just sorry for all the people he owed money to, for they'll never see it now.''

"And then there's Lord Byron. What a good thing it was that he had already left England before Caroline Lamb brought out her novel, *Glenarvon,*'' Lady Casterfield said, "or he might well have murdered her.''

"Oh, I don't think he'd go to such extremes, Muriel. I always felt he had an excellent sense of humor and was, in fact, quite patient as far as Caroline was concerned. It's her husband that I'm sorry for. I've heard that some of his friends say he must leave her or everyone will think he had something to do with the book's publication.'' Lady Fitzwilliam shook her head sadly.

Sir George, who had been listening quietly to the ladies' gossip while keeping an eye out for anything untoward happening, decided it was time he added a word. "It would be the best thing for him if he broke the relationship completely. That young man had a very promising career until her scandalous behavior forced him out of politics. He should leave her and pick up where he left off,'' he said firmly.

Lady Fitzwilliam turned around and gave him a bright smile. "I think I agree with you, George,'' she said, "for he has been extremely patient with her and I, for one, do not believe for a moment that he had anything to do with publishing the book. She clearly portrayed him as a most unsavory character in it.''

"Then you have read the book, already, Gertrude?" Lady Casterfield asked.

"Of course I have, Muriel," Lady Fitzwilliam snapped. "I do try to keep myself abreast of things that are going on, you know. George has read it also, haven't you, my dear?"

"Certainly I have, for I wouldn't think to offer criticism had I not read it. The person to whom Caroline has been the most insulting, however, is her mother-in-law, Lady Melbourne. She shows a most distasteful feeling of relish as she describes how that lady is stabbed to death," Sir George asserted.

Lady Eversly and Lady Casterfield looked quite stunned by this revelation. To break the silence, Lady Fitzwilliam asked Sir George, "Did Arabella and Miles decide to play a few hands of cards?"

"I really don't know, but you can be sure they will be joining us soon at supper," he told her meaningfully, for it would not do for him to admit before the others that he had seen the young couple entering a small side room alone.

Lady Fitzwilliam nodded, guessing where they might be. She had no reservations on this score, for anyone with eyes in their face could tell that Miles was still in love with Arabella and meant to marry her this time. In any case, in view of the threats, it was best that he was never far from her niece's side.

Lady Eversly rose to attend to her neglected duties as hostess, and the others strolled over to greet other longtime friends and eventually settled down for a couple of friendly hands of cards.

Miles caught a glimpse of his uncle and waved as he and Arabella strolled into the small family portrait gallery. The only other couple there quickly left, and then they had the place to themselves.

They slowly walked around, discussing the Eversly ancestors and the merits of the artists who had painted them, then Miles took Arabella's hand in his. Now was the time for another foray.

"Have you given any further consideration to my proposal

of marriage, my dear?'' he asked gently. ''I do not intend to take no for an answer, you know, for I believe you have more feelings for me now than you had the last time, isn't that true?''

Arabella's cheeks turned pink and she nodded. ''Of course I'm fond of you,'' she admitted in a whisper, looking toward the door to be sure no one was near enough to hear. ''I was before, but then I was just a silly little girl and didn't know what life was all about.''

''I'm going to keep asking you until I wear you down and you finally agree,'' he told her, putting a hand on her waist and turning her so that his broad shoulders shielded her from the view of anyone passing the door.

One of the fingers of his other hand was feathering across her cheek so gently that it scarcely touched the skin, but it still caused a rush of warmth to spread through her body and make her feel excitingly alive. She started to close her eyes lest they reveal to him just how she really felt.

''Open your eyes,'' he ordered a little hoarsely, and as she automatically complied, he added, ''for whatever your lips might say, your eyes never lie to me. Do you know that they go a deeper blue when your emotions are aroused?''

She shook her head slightly, then started to tremble as his finger started to slowly circle the edges of her mouth. Did he have any idea, she wondered, how much she wanted to feel his lips where his finger strayed?

There was a discreet cough from the direction of the door, then Sir George's voice called, a little too loudly, ''So there you are. Will you join us, for we're just going to supper?''

Miles heaved a sigh, then grinned down at Arabella, releasing her waist and offering his arm. ''Shall we, my dear?'' he asked, and too breathless to answer, she just nodded.

''A handsome lot, the Eversly ancestors, aren't they?'' Sir George asked, grinning as Arabella and Miles came out of the gallery.

''To be honest, they're not really at all good-looking until you come to the present generation,'' Miles said smoothly, glancing around to be sure none of them was nearby. "The last earl's mother was a beauty, and she has made a vast improvement in the strain."

"How strange," Sir George remarked. "I never noticed and I'm usually more observant than that."

Lady Fitzwilliam had taken Arabella by the hand. "I don't think we should stay long after we have eaten supper, my love, for after your not feeling well yesterday, I believe you should have a fairly early night. You look a bit flushed now, as a matter of fact."

Knowing the cause, Arabella immediately went even pinker, but she much preferred to leave when there was a crowd going at the same time, so she readily agreed. Despite their good intentions, however, it was still more than two hours before Miles spoke to a footman and asked him to have their carriage sent around.

The call down the Bear and Ragged Staff Mews for the Warrington coach was loud and clear, but it came at a time when a number of other carriages had been called for and were blocking the way.

"It'll be a good fifteen to twenty minutes before we can get through that lot," Tom Coachman told Ben. "We've time for another 'and or two."

As they settled down to finish their game, none of them noticed the old drunk who made his unsteady passage behind their coach and passed the last of the ones waiting in line. Had Ben been facing that way, he undoubtedly would have seen him, but as it happened, his back was toward the coach for the minute or so it took the man to get beyond it.

When the drunk reached the coach that would be two ahead of the Warrington one, he paused. He really did not know what he was going to do, for he preferred to wait and take advantage of whatever opportunity arose. His pistol, all ready to fire, was in a holster beneath his jacket, and up his sleeve was a small, quite deadly dagger. But he might not use either of these weapons—and then again he might use one or both.

The coachman's estimate was not quite accurate, for there was a delay while one coach ahead had to wait for a young lady's reticule to be brought from where she had left it. And then a party realized at the last minute that the head of the house was still in a card room. He heard Tom Coachman's fluent curses at the delays as he stepped on a coach a little ahead and got himself a free ride into Curzon Street, dropping off at the corner and falling back once more into the shadows to creep closer to the Everslys' house.

They were there, all four of them waiting outside, for the night was warm and pleasant. Miles Cavendish was standing quite close to the Barton widow, yet not touching her.

The drunk slid along silently until he was almost directly behind her, then he looked up as he heard something in the distance. A carriage, probably in the hands of some young buck, was racing along Curzon Street from the direction of Lansdowne House. From where he was standing at the back, he could clearly see the carriage and four horses, but it was blocked from the view of the party he was watching by the next coach in line, taking on its passengers.

He smiled unpleasantly. It would take careful timing, but he was sure he could do it with seconds to spare.

He counted, one, two, three, and then he leapt forward, grasped Arabella by the waist, and pushed her along, to fling her down in the road in front of the oncoming carriage. As he had expected, his own momentum carried him to safety on the other side of the street, and he leapt for the railings that enclosed the grounds of Chesterfield House. Once again he could easily give any pursuer the slip.

It was fortunate that Miles was fully alert to danger only seconds before Arabella was attacked. He felt the rush of air as she was swept completely off her feet and flung in the path of the carriage, and he was only a second behind.

Concentrating only on saving her, he threw himself forward, not stopping until he had pushed her beyond the reach of the oncoming horses' hooves. The impact knocked the wind out of both of them, so that he lay for a moment, on top of her, trying to catch his breath.

The street was in an uproar. The carriage had managed to stop some distance beyond them, and the driver was being soundly berated for traveling at such a speed, and somewhere to the north side of the street he could hear Ben's voice and also that of Sir George, and he vaguely wondered what they were doing.

Then Lady Fitzwilliam was bending over Arabella. "My dear, are you all right?" she asked. "How very foolish of me to ask such a question. Of course you're not all right—nor is Miles, by the look of it, but he undoubtedly saved your life."

Arabella was shaking as she scrambled away from Miles and started to get up. She felt hurt and bruised all over, but her legs did not give way until she turned and saw the man who had just tried to kill her, being securely held by Ben and Sir George. All of a sudden, her knees buckled and she sank to the ground again.

Ted came hurrying over. "Are you all right, milord?" he asked Miles, who had not yet made any attempt to rise.

"Of course," Miles said tersely. "Just a little winded, that's all. If our carriage is here, help the ladies into it. Would you mind taking Arabella home and getting her to bed, Lady Fitzwilliam?" he asked. "Now that we've finally caught him, George and I need to have a word with that blackguard before we put him in the hands of the authorities. The carriage can take you first and then come back for us."

As they started to cross the street, he called Ted back and said quietly, "My cane is inside the carriage. Bring it over here before you leave."

"Yes, milord," Ted said, eyeing him sharply and receiving an angry glare in return.

It was a very thoughtful Arabella who allowed herself to be assisted into the coach, then sat beside her aunt for the drive home. Ben was one of her aunt's servants, yet he was behaving as though he worked for Miles and Sir George.

And what was that Miles had said? Now that we've finally caught him, wasn't it? That meant he'd been trying to catch him before, but why would he be doing that when he knew nothing about the threats?

In the park this morning Ben and Miles had been looking

at the man on horseback under a tree, and talking as though they knew each other well. He must have told Miles about what happened the night of the royal wedding.

When she got back to her aunt's house, she meant to have a word with Dora. She'd never seemed the type of girl who couldn't keep a secret, but she meant to find out before her head hit the pillow.

"You must be feeling quite dreadful, my dear," Lady Fitzwilliam said softly. "I think that as soon as we get home, we must get you into a warm bath and find out the extent of your injuries. It's quite possible that you are more seriously hurt than you realize. I do hope your papa is not home yet, for he'll be beside himself if he sees you in this condition."

"I'm all right, but I agree that a warm bath would be most helpful. I was trying to get up, you know, when Miles dragged me out of the way, but I know I'd never have succeeded. That man was actually trying to kill me," she said in a voice filled with horror.

Lady Fitzwilliam reached over and patted her niece's hand. "I know, my dear, for I was standing there watching the whole thing and completely unable to do anything to stop it. I know he made threats, but I never for a moment realized that he meant to kill you."

Arabella looked at her aunt in surprise. "You knew about the threats, Aunt Gertrude? Who told you?"

It was obvious that her aunt realized she'd said too much from the way she became so flustered. "Did I say threats? Well, I must have been thinking of something else. I really don't know," she tried to say; then, seeing Arabella's look of disbelief, she told her, "Miles told me just the other day. He felt I should be aware of it."

"And how did Miles find out?" Arabella asked. "I certainly did not tell him . . . or anyone else."

Then she remembered Dora, the maid who was very intelligent yet said she couldn't read and who was very friendly with Ben, her aunt's groom, who seemed to know Miles Cavendish very well indeed. Didn't she once say that her last position had been in a house where two bachelors lived?

Dora was going to answer a lot of questions this evening and she would probably give her the scold of her life—and tomorrow Arabella would deal with Miles Cavendish.

18

Under Arabella's stern questioning, Dora broke down and admitted that she had worked for Miles and his family ever since she was a little girl. She could, of course, both read and write, and had made copies of all the threatening notes and sent them to him.

"Why did you come here in the first place?" Arabella asked as she soaked her bruised body in the steaming, rose-scented water. "You and Ben started working here about the same time, didn't you, as I arrived in London?"

Tearfully, Dora admitted as much.

"What were you supposed to do, Dora, spy on me? And to what purpose?" Arabella snapped.

"All we were to do was let Lord Cavendish know where you and Lady Fitzwilliam meant to be each night, nothing more," Dora said. "I didn't say a word about our going to the royal wedding. It was Ben who told him about that, and the master was so angry with me for leading you into danger that I think he would have dismissed me had I not been working for you. And after being with the family since I was a little tweeny and my pa was head footman.

"I'd have done anything to make it right with him again, so when I saw that note, I knew if I copied it and sent it to him

203

it would put me back in his good graces. Ben said there must be more, so I looked and found the others and copied them as well, then he took them to the master. Ben was his batman in the army.''

"I see," Arabella said tightly. "I think it's absolutely despicable that someone would place spies in another person's house to pry into their personal habits and affairs."

Dora looked miserable. "It wasn't like that, milady, really it wasn't," she said, wringing her hands. "I wouldn't have spied on you."

"Then why did you search my things for those letters?" Arabella asked tartly. "Do you do everything Ben tells you to?"

"You looked so frightened and I knew the master would want to help, milady," the girl tried to explain, but tonight her mistress was too angry to even try to understand.

Arabella put out a hand for a towel. "You can help me out of here and then I'm going to get into bed and sleep on it. I've only acted in haste once in my whole life, and I'm not going to do that again. You can take out my green walking gown and be sure it's pressed and mended, for I'll be going to see your master first thing in the morning, and don't you dare let him know I'm coming."

But Dora did dare, for though she had become fond of Lady Arabella, her first loyalty would always be to the family who had been so good to her. Even before Arabella awoke, Dora sent a note to Lord Cavendish letting him know to expect a very angry visitor.

Miles was awake when the note arrived. He had scarcely slept all night, for his leg was giving him too much pain. On the pretext of doing some paperwork, he had stayed up until after Sir George had retired for the night, and had then sent for Ted and Ben to help him up the stairs. He had intended, first thing this morning, to send for Dr. Radcliff, but then Dora's note had arrived and his plans were quickly changed.

After a frugal breakfast in bed, he waited with some impatience for his uncle to go and see the magistrate and lay formal charges against the man who had tried to kill

Arabella. George had been in an expansive mood, happy that the whole affair had reached a satisfactory conclusion and in no hurry to rush off at what he termed crack of dawn but to Miles was after nine o'clock.

But he left at last, and the minute the door closed after him, Miles had ordered his valet to help him get dressed to go downstairs, but this was not as easy to do as it sounded. To don morning dress while seated on the edge of the bed, or propped against it, was a task that called for more patience than Miles possessed.

Eventually, however, he looked reasonably presentable, so Ted and a particularly strong groom were summoned to carry him down the stairs and help him into the large chair behind his desk in the study. While he waited for Arabella to arrive, he penned a note to Dr. Radcliff asking if he could do him the favor of calling on him here this afternoon.

Not fifteen minutes after the note had been sent to the doctor, Arabella was at the door, accompanied by Dora.

She left the maid in the hall, then almost stormed into the study while a footman hurried after her to place a chair for her in front of the desk.

The door had scarcely closed behind the footman before Arabella began, "I have never heard of anything so despicable in all my life, sir. To place spies in the home of my aunt, one of the most esteemed ladies of the *ton*, is outrageous."

"How are you feeling this morning, my dear?" Miles asked quietly. "That's a nasty bruise on your forehead. Did you experience any other ill effects from being handled so roughly?"

Arabella looked startled, for she had expected him to go immediately on the defensive. "I have a lot of other bruises besides this one," she admitted grudgingly, "and I am a little stiff, but otherwise I'm all right."

"I'm very pleased to hear it, and I hope you slept well last night and did not suffer from nightmares," he added.

"The only nightmares I suffered were because of your outrageous behavior," she almost screamed at him, then turned to look guiltily at the door as though she expected someone to come running in to see what was happening.

"It's quite all right, Arabella. The door and walls are extremely thick and rarely can anything be heard outside," Miles said with a faint smile.

He's being disarming and I won't have it, Arabella said to herself. She went on, "There I thought it mere coincidence that you and Sir George appeared at every social occasion we attended, and now I find that it was planned all the time," she said, her voice rising once more. "Have you no conscience? Didn't you feel the slightest guilt that you were invading my privacy?"

"But I did not invade your privacy, Arabella, and I'm sure Dora did not tell you that I did. Have you any idea how many social affairs are held every evening in this city? It would have been impossible to have seen you more than once a week had I left it to mere chance," he explained apologetically. "And I saw no reason to take that kind of risk. Not when I wanted to marry you."

If he had been able to rise from behind the desk, he would have taken her in his arms and comforted her, for he knew she was angry only because she was hurt by his behavior. For just a moment she looked lonely and quite vulnerable, then it was gone.

"You may not have actually asked Ben about the incident near Carlton House, but the fact that he was your man gave you access to private information about me that I would never have wanted you to have," she said a little more quietly.

Now Miles did smile, if a little grimly. "Do you realize that you would not even be here to talk about it if Ben had not been my man and, because he was concerned on my behalf, had followed you? I think you will admit now that he saved your life on that occasion. Your enemy was not playing games but was going for the jugular," he said, a touch impatiently.

Arabella had the grace to flush.

"I was completely shocked that you had been so foolish as to even consider the suggestion that he might get you in to see the wedding. Surely you know that, with only fifty people invited, a stranger would have stood out at once and would probably have been arrested,'' Miles said, sounding a little disgusted.

Then he realized that this would never achieve his objective and that a tactical withdrawal was called for, but how to do that when he could not even stand up was another matter.

A loud knock sounded on the door, and his butler entered. ''Dr. Radcliff is here to see you, sir,'' he said firmly, quite obviously of the opinion that this visitor was more important than the young lady.

''Tell him . . .'' Miles began when Tom Radcliff walked in, his bag in his hand.

''Tell him what, Miles?'' he asked as the butler withdrew. ''I came now because I have surgery to perform this afternoon. What did you do to your leg?''

''Oh, no,'' Arabella gasped, her eyes suddenly filled with concern.

''I believe you met Lady Arabella Barton on a previous occasion, Tom,'' Miles said gravely, wondering what to do, for though he was badly in need of Tom's help, he still hoped to become reconciled with Arabella. She got up as though to leave, and he tried to rise also, but the pain was too severe.

''Dr. Radcliff, Miles, I'll see you later,'' she said softly, and walked quickly from the room, closely followed by the doctor, who called loudly, ''I need a couple of strong footmen in here to give me a hand.''

Arabella gave a little gasp, then sat down next to Dora, determined to wait.

''Now, let's see what this is all about,'' Tom said to Miles, showing the men exactly how to lift their master while he himself carefully cradled the bad leg. ''Over here on this couch will do nicely, and I think we'll ease the trousers off before you set him down. It's a good thing you didn't try to put on breeches this morning, Miles, or we'd have had to cut them off.''

When he saw the bare leg, swollen and covered in bruises and scrapes, he gave a low whistle and then dismissed the footmen.

''This must have been quite a fall. What happened?'' he asked.

"I might as well tell you the truth, for I imagine you'll hear some version of it soon enough, as it happened in front of a great many members of the *ton*. A villain tried to kill Arabella by pushing her in front of a fast-moving coach. I leapt after her and managed to push us both to safety, but I went down hard and I think I may have torn a few things in that leg, for it's giving me the very deuce of a time," Miles explained, gasping as Tom bent over the leg, his skillful fingers searching for signs of damage.

"You certainly didn't help it to heal, Miles, but you may not have damaged it as badly as you think," Tom told him as he continued to poke and probe. "If you'll stop trying to put weight on it and going up and down stairs for a few days, it's possible that I may not have to go in again. I'll give you something to ease the pain, and I know I don't have to tell you to be careful how you take it."

He straightened up. "I'll stop by again tomorrow to see how it's feeling, and you'll have to let those footmen carry you up the stairs unless you want to set up a bed down here."

There was a knock on the door and, to Miles' relief, the butler handed in a blanket with which to cover him.

When Tom Radcliff stepped into the hall a few minutes later, he was not at all surprised to see that Lady Arabella had waited. "He's going to be all right, I believe, if he keeps off it now for a while," he told her. "How about you? I'm sure that bruise on your head is not the only one you suffered."

"Of course not," she agreed ruefully. "I feel as though I fell off a galloping horse onto a very hard road, but there are no bones broken and I know I'm extremely lucky to be alive. But I didn't even thank him for saving me."

"Well, he won't want to see you again right now in his present state of dishabille, so I suggest you give him a day or two to rest and then he'll be in much better condition to receive your thanks," he said with a grin, "for I know that's how I would feel."

"But I was dreadfully angry and screaming at him," Arabella protested a little tearfully.

"Write him a letter, then," the doctor suggested. "But

don't scream in it, for goodness sake, for screams always sound louder in letters. Write something that will make him smile, or, better still, laugh. You should have seen the faces of wounded soldiers when they got a cheerful letter from a wife or best girl.''

"Thank you, Doctor, I'll follow your advice,'' she said with a smile, having taken an instant liking to him. "Come along, Dora,'' she called, and they started back to Hanover Square.

"Arabella, where on earth have you been?'' Lady Fitzwilliam asked when her niece came into the study. "After what happened last night, you couldn't possibly be in any fit condition to go out this morning.''

Arabella looked at her with a strange expression on her face. "I wanted to tell Miles exactly what I thought about him,'' she said quietly. "So I went to his house and I ranted and raved at him, and I had no idea that he was sitting there in terrible pain because he hurt his leg in saving me.''

"Oh, dear,'' Lady Fitzwilliam frowned. "I was afraid something like that had happened last night when he did not get up right away. But I cannot think why you should be angry with someone who saved your life. You didn't quarrel with him this morning, did you, my dear?''

"No, but it wasn't for lack of trying. He just wouldn't get angry,'' Arabella said, not wishing her aunt to know any more about her activities than she did already.

"Was Sir George present during your tirade?'' Lady Fitzwilliam asked, suddenly realizing what her niece had done.

"I didn't see him,'' Arabella said, "so I assumed that he was out.''

Her aunt looked at her questioningly. "Are you telling me that you went to visit a gentleman at his bachelor residence without a chaperon, and with not even another gentleman present?''

"I took Dora with me, of course, but made her wait in the hall,'' Arabella said, then admitted, "I suppose it wasn't really the thing to do, but I just had to see him and tell him what I thought of his behavior.''

Lady Fitzwilliam frowned. "Other than his servants, did

anyone see you go in or out of the house?'' she asked.

"Only Dr. Radcliff. Miles must have sent for him, but did not expect him until this afternoon,'' Arabella said by way of explanation.

Her aunt sighed heavily. "If anyone else saw you, you could be in serious trouble, for word of what happened last night may already have spread like wildfire. If your reputation is further damaged, Miles may decide not to propose marriage, you know.''

"He has already done so twice, Aunt Gertrude, yesterday morning and then last night in the Everslys' portrait gallery,'' Arabella told her, unable to hide a tiny feeling of triumph.

"And that's another thing I was going to talk to you about, Arabella. Last night you . . .'' Lady Fitzwilliam stopped, realizing that her niece had told her that Miles had actually proposed. "Why did he need to ask twice? Don't tell me you didn't accept him the first time?'' she asked in amazement. "You'll never find a man like him again, and I know he loves you dearly.''

"I had my reasons,'' Arabella said sharply, a little put out at being questioned so. "And now, if you will excuse me, I must go upstairs and write a letter.''

But try as she might, Arabella could not compose the kind of letter she wanted to write to Miles. As the day went along and she realized that she no longer had any anonymous notes to worry about and was free to allow her true feelings to surface, she alternated between dreaming of a future that definitely included Miles Cavendish and resigning herself to one where she kept house for her father and grew older and older as she entertained his friends and looked after Snowball.

In the end, she picked up a pen and wrote, "How sharper than a serpent's tooth it is to have a thankless friend! Please let me know when you are well enough to have visitors. Arabella.''

Even if she had wished to do so, she could not have gone out that evening, for the bruise on her forehead had become so dark that it could not possibly be hidden.

Lord Darnley, who had been completely shocked when

he heard of the attack on his daughter, had decided to stay home also and give her a game of chess—after she told him just what had been going on.

Sir George arrived after dinner to escort Lady Fitzwilliam to a theater party and told them of his meeting with the magistrate that morning when he brought formal charges against Viscount Alexander Galbraith for the attempted murder of Arabella.

"He has apparently made no effort to deny the charges and has, in fact, admitted that this was not his first attempt upon your life, Arabella," Sir George said quietly. "I promise you that it will, however, be his last."

"Has word of it got around as yet?" Lady Fitzwilliam asked him.

"Surprisingly, it has not, for I don't think even the people who saw something realized exactly what had happened," Sir George said. "I heard a rumor that two people had been crossing Curzon Street and had been almost killed by runaway horses, and that may be as far as it will go."

"That's what I heard, too," Lord Darnley told him.

"It's bound to come out when the case comes before a judge if, as you say, the man is of noble birth," Lady Fitzwilliam said, "but by then it may be almost the end of the Season."

"Did this viscount give any real reason for wishing to kill me?" Arabella asked. "His first note said he was glad about Richard's death, and the next one said my enticements were to blame, which was nonsense, for I was most circumspect. And to blame for what?"

Sir George looked surprised, for he had thought Miles would have told her everything this morning when she had gone to see him, but if he had not, then she had a right to know.

"You may be sure Miles did not let the authorities have the man until he had forced out of him the reasons for seeking revenge against you," he began, wishing Miles had taken care of this also. "Apparently, his younger brother, a Timothy Galbraith, lost badly at Richard's hands. It was a considerable sum—money and estates worth twenty thousand pounds—and he swore to Galbraith that he had been cheated, though he said he couldn't prove it.''

"I remember him," Arabella said softly, "for it wasn't often that Richard made such a big win. I never knew his name, but he was very young, and to Richard's delight, he kept watching me instead of keeping his mind on the game. I left the room once, but Richard came after me and forced me to come back.''

Sir George nodded, then said quietly, "The morning after he'd told his brother of his loss, Galbraith found him. He'd killed himself.''

"Oh, no!" Arabella's eyes filled with tears and she reached for a kerchief. "He was such a nice, gentle sort of young man, and he looked as though he'd only just started to shave," she said, trying to hold back a sob.

Lady Fitzwilliam came over and put an arm around her shoulders, but Arabella shook her head. "No, Aunt Gertrude, please leave me alone. It's just too dreadful. That poor boy.''

"It would have been even more dreadful if his brother had succeeded in killing you for that poor boy's death," her aunt said a little tartly. "I'm sure his losing was no fault of yours.''

"No, it wasn't," Arabella agreed, "for I did all I could to stop distracting him from the game. It went on for two days, and I put scarves and fichus into the necklines of my gowns to cover myself up as much as I could.''

Sir George nodded. "I'm sure you didn't realize it but sometimes that's more enticing than leaving the neck bare," he told her. "Barques of frailty do that so that their gentlemen can have the pleasure of pulling out the fichus for themselves.''

Arabella looked across at her father, who nodded in agreement.

"I am quite sure that it was none of your fault, my dear," he said. "I wonder why Galbraith didn't take revenge on Richard?''

"He meant to," Sir George told him, "but by the time he buried his brother and found out where Richard had gone to next, it was too late. He said he arrived only in time to see Richard being accused of cheating and killed in the duel."

There was silence for a few moments, then Lady Fitzwilliam said, "I think we'd best be leaving, George," and she got up to go.

At the door Sir George remembered that he had brought with him Miles' reply, and he turned back to give it to Arabella with a murmured, "Now don't you keep fretting about this. It was none of it your fault."

Her face brightened when she saw the letter, and excusing herself to her father, she opened it right away. It read, "Friendship is constant in all other things save in the office and affairs of love. I do not want you to be but a friend, thankless or not. Miles."

Arabella slept soundly that night. She had told her father much, if not all, of what had been happening, and he had scolded her severely for keeping it from him. After that he had beaten her soundly at chess, while admitting that it was a little unfair, for her mind had not really been on the game.

She looked well rested when Dora brought her hot chocolate the next morning. "Come back in a half-hour and I will have a note for you to take to your master," she told her. The maid was relieved to see that she was smiling happily.

When the maid had gone, Arabella took her chocolate over to the escritoire and unfolded Miles' last note. After reading it again, she penned her reply: "I feared my ranting might have torn your passion to tatters, to very rags. Can you bear to see me if I call tomorrow to try to repair it? Arabella."

After allowing Dora to dress her, she sent her off with the note, then proceeded to brush her own hair and tie it back with a ribbon that matched her gown, all the while humming softly to herself as she worked.

She and her aunt met at the head of the stairs, and Lady Fitzwilliam stopped to take a look at her niece. "That's good," she said, "though the bruise seems to have become even darker, you appear to be in the most remarkable spirits, considering all that has happened."

"I am," Arabella said, smiling and slipping her hand through her aunt's arm. "Come along, for I feel as though I haven't eaten for a week."

But when she was only halfway through a most substantial breakfast, the doorbell sounded.

"Who could that be at this hour?" Lady Fitzwilliam asked, but her frown of annoyance quickly left as she heard Sir George's voice in the hall.

A moment later he entered, bowed low over Lady Fitzwilliam's hand, then turned and wagged a finger at Arabella. "You, young lady, have turned our entire household upside down in a matter of minutes," he said, trying to look severe. "My nephew insists that he must see you tomorrow. He has ordered that the study be cleaned from floor to ceiling, for he absolutely refuses to entertain a lady in either his bedchamber again or in a room that smells of dusty books."

Lady Fitzwilliam looked at him in surprise, then said, "You surely have time to join us for some breakfast, Sir George, and to tell me, if not my niece, what this is all about."

Dawson, who had been standing by, set a place for him at once, then left the room, closing the door firmly behind him.

"If I may help myself to some of this excellent-looking fare, I'll explain why I'm here at this early hour, my lady," Sir George told her as he quickly filled a plate. He took his seat, then reached for the cup of coffee Arabella had poured for him.

Lady Fitzwilliam glanced at her niece, but Arabella appeared to be quite fascinated with the design of the wallpaper, for she was looking at it as if she had never seen it before.

"Whatever you put in that note, young lady, I sincerely hope you meant it, for I've not seen Miles look so well and happy since the old days when his father was alive." Sir George gave Arabella a warning look.

"It was a private letter," Arabella told him sternly, though the corners of her mouth twitched a little, "and I most certainly did mean every word of it."

"Then may I assume that you two ladies will pay us a call tomorrow morning about eleven o'clock, for I'm sure that by then he will be safely ensconced in a spotless study, looking for all the world as if he'd had nothing to do with that miraculous rescue the other night?" He turned to Lady Fitzwilliam and slowly closed one eye.

She smiled at him. "Of course, we will, won't we, Arabella?"

"Only on one consideration, Aunt Gertrude," Arabella said firmly. "That I may see Miles completely alone, in the study, if that is where he will be."

"Well, as long as the door is open—" her aunt began.

"With the door closed tightly," Arabella insisted, "or I will not come. I am not a chit fresh from the schoolroom, and you will just have to trust us both, that's all."

Lady Fitzwilliam looked at Sir George, her eyebrows raised.

"He'll not harm a hair on her head," he assured her, then chuckled. "But as for you being left alone with me in the drawing room, now that's another matter entirely, my lady."

19

Arabella and Lady Fitzwilliam arrived promptly at Miles' house at eleven o'clock and were shown into the drawing room, where Sir George arose to greet them.

"Miles is awaiting you in the study, my dear," he told Arabella. "He said that you know where it is and are to go straight in."

She thanked him, then went out into the hall and toward the study, but she had thought the door would be open. When it was not, she hesitated, wondering whether to knock and, if she did, would he hear her?

Of course he wouldn't, she decided, for wasn't the door so thick as to make the room soundproof?

Taking a deep breath, she grasped the knob, turned it, and pushed open the heavy door.

She had expected to see him sitting behind the desk, but when there was nothing but a huge, empty chair facing the door, she was surprised for a moment.

"Do come in, Arabella, and close the door behind you. And please forgive me for not rising." Miles' voice came from one end of the couch beneath the window, but the sunlight behind him made it difficult for her to make out much of him save the outline of his head. Then she saw the hand he was holding out, and she went forward and clasped it between both of hers.

His outstretched leg was supported by a well-padded chair, and he indicated the space next to him on the couch. "Won't you join me? I ran out of apt quotations," he said, smiling gently, "but, I, also, wanted to see you."

Arabella's cheeks went a bright pink and she sat down on the couch as far away from him as she could.

"How is your leg?" she asked a little breathlessly.

"My leg is coming along very well, my dear, but I believe this is the first time in ages that I have seen you at a loss for words," Miles said with some amusement. "It's interesting, but I've grown to appreciate your forthright manner of speaking. What on earth is the matter with you?"

"I'm embarrassed because I berated you so when your leg was paining you like that," Arabella told him.

He looked surprised. "You are? I don't see how one thing has anything to do with the other. Had you been embarrassed at some of the things you said to me, then that I might have understood. I thought I had understood, in fact, for in one of the quotations I do recall that you were anxious to repair my passion?"

This was not at all how she had expected either one of them to behave. Had he, perhaps, decided he no longer wished to marry her? She decided a change of subject might help.

"Sir George told us why Viscount Galbraith wanted to get revenge, and in a way I can understand, for his brother was very young," she said. "Is he sorry now for what he tried to do to me?"

Miles shook his head. "I don't believe so. I think he has become a little deranged, my dear, for he never had a logical reason for killing you. Now, if he'd just wanted to kill Richard, it would have made some sense."

"What will happen to him now?" she asked.

"That may depend on you," Miles told her. "He readily admits to what he tried to do, so he could be hanged. However, I think that his young brother's suicide has affected his mind and it might be kinder to put him in an asylum for the mentally deranged."

Arabella thought about it for a moment. "Is that really kinder?" she asked. "I think I would rather die than spend the rest of my life in such a place. How does it depend on me? I don't have to see him again, do I?"

"That's up to the judge. He may wish to know your feelings in the matter. And then it depends on whether or not Galbraith has any influential friends. But let's talk about something a little more cheerful," he suggested. "Did your aunt accompany you this time?"

Now Arabella was really breathless; her heart felt as though it might pound its way right through her chest. Looking into his eyes, she nodded slowly, then suddenly his arm came around her, sweeping her up and pressing her close to him.

"I think we're ready now to make a start on repairing that passion, my love, don't you?" he murmured as his lips traced a pattern from her throat to her mouth, where they settled for what promised to be an extended stay.

Arabella could not have replied if she'd wanted to, and she forgot all about her former nervousness as she was swept up into sensations more wonderful than she'd ever felt before. Nothing in the world mattered now as much as the feel of his strong arms about her and the desire that was racing through her, sweeping everything else away before it. There was no past, only the present in Miles' arms, and as his kiss deepened, she felt as though nothing bad could ever happen to her again.

As for Miles, he couldn't get enough of her. She tasted like nothing he could name, yet he knew it to be a flavor he could never live without again. He wanted all of her quite desperately, yet he knew he must wait, must not frighten her, for, despite her years of marriage, he could tell that she'd never known a passion like the one they were sharing now could exist.

Slowly, tenderly, he drew his lips away from hers and felt rather than heard her soft moan at the loss. As his mouth now traced delicate patterns on her temples, her cheeks, her eyes, her sigh of contentment was like a soft breath that lightly fanned his face.

"I have to ask the question again, my love, for you indicated you might say yes but did not say the actual word," he murmured softly. "You do intend to make an honest man of me, don't you?"

"Oh, yes, please," she breathed, "and the sooner I do, the happier I'll be, for I don't want to stop doing this, and I know we must."

His lips were against her temple and he could smell the scent of rose petals and lavender as he said, "I'll get a special license, for we've both waited long enough. We can be married in your aunt's house, if she doesn't mind."

Suddenly there was a loud banging on the door and then a pause that gave them time enough to spring apart, but not to lose the look of being in love.

Lady Fitzwilliam entered first, closely followed by Sir George.

As they walked over toward the window, Lady Fitzwilliam smiled and Arabella realized that she suddenly looked at least ten years younger.

"Gertrude has just accepted my proposal of marriage," Sir George told Miles and Arabella, "and I'm going to get a special license so that we can tie the knot as quickly as possible."

As Arabella jumped up to throw her arms around her aunt, Miles said to his uncle, his eyes twinkling, "How very convenient, George, for you can get one for me at the same time. Allow me to congratulate you and wish you every happiness."

"Thank you, my boy," Sir George said, grasping the younger man's outstretched hand. "Am I to understand that the colonel's campaign was successful?"

"Completely, sir."

The older man nodded. "I never doubted you for a moment, but I believe that particular foray had best be kept between the two of us?" he suggested, raising an eyebrow.

"Decidedly," Miles replied with a broad wink, "decidedly, sir."

ROMANTIC ENCOUNTERS

By the year 2000, 2 out of 3 Americans could be illiterate.

It's true.

Today, 75 million adults...about one American in three, can't read adequately. And by the year 2000, U.S. News & World Report envisions an America with a literacy rate of only 30%.

Before that America comes to be, you can stop it...by joining the fight against illiteracy today.

Call the Coalition for Literacy at toll-free **1-800-228-8813** and volunteer.

Volunteer Against Illiteracy. The only degree you need is a degree of caring.